HOT *Italian* NIGHTS

BOOKS 1 to 3

ANNIE WEST

Cover Design and Interior Format

BACK IN THE
Italian's Bed

Book 1, Hot Italian Nights

*For the very special friends who helped
me with Fabrizio and Jenna's story:
Karen, Reeze, Vanessa and Serena.
With thanks and love.*

Chapter One

'WELCOME, SIGNOR ARMATI.'

Fabrizio strode past the bowing lawyer and into the conference room of his Rome headquarters. His eyes locked with those of his rival on the far side of the vast table.

Luca De Laurentis. The man had been snapping at his heels for years and just twelve months ago had beaten him to the lucrative Palermo deal. He'd been a thorn in Fabrizio's side for too long.

Satisfaction stirred. At last their cat and mouse game neared its end and he, Fabrizio Armati, would emerge the victor. He tasted triumph on his tongue. After the trying six months he'd had, the promise of success had never been so sweet.

'De Laurentis.' He nodded, noting the glint in his competitor's eye, as if ready for battle. Much good it would do him. Fabrizio's team had the deal sewn up to his complete satisfaction. He intended to leave the room with everything he wanted.

'Armati.' De Laurentis inclined his head and settled in his seat, surrounded by dark-suited minions.

Fabrizio took the chair reserved for him at the head of his own entourage and leaned back, ready to enjoy himself.

It was as his chief lawyer opened the sheaf of contracts on the table that Fabrizio felt a ripple of disquiet, a feather of awareness along his nape. The blood in his veins tingled. His nostrils flared as if scenting some half-forgotten fragrance. His skin tightened.

Slowly, casually, he turned from the papers and swept his gaze over the opposition ranks. Half-familiar faces were already frowning over the latest proposals. Grey hair, balding heads, De Laurentis's carefully groomed dark hair, more forgettable faces and then, at the back, half-obscured by the men in front, a face he'd never forget.

Jenna MacDonald.

His shuffle of the papers before him cloaked a swift intake of breath.

The ripple of disquiet became a sizzle of pure fire, searing through his blood and igniting a fury he'd barely managed to contain in twenty-six weeks.

Twenty-six weeks since he'd seen her.

Six months since he'd opened that trite little note.

One hundred and eighty-two days since he'd left her sleeping in his bed, her hair catching the dawn light like gold caught the sun.

Fabrizio's lip curled in a snarl of indignation. Never in his life had he counted the days with a woman. But he knew precisely how long he'd been *without* Jenna MacDonald.

She was the only woman in thirty-three years to walk away from him.

Maledizione! To find her here of all places, after he'd sent his investigators overseas to locate her!

He firmed his mouth into a hard line. What game was this?

He took in her sleek hair, pulled back from her

exquisite face. Those siren's lips in glossy carmine. The charcoal jacket that plunged low over a silky cream camisole. The way her throat worked as she swallowed.

Fabrizio's eyes narrowed as he saw her pulse flutter. She was nervous.

So she damned well should be! She was lucky he didn't stalk over there and haul her out into the open rather than let her skulk among De Laurentis's yes men.

As if sensing his stare, her eyes flicked up and caught on his. The impact of that aquamarine gaze carved a familiar hollow through his chest.

Fury, he assured himself.

Anger at her betrayal.

Righteous affront at being left by his lover without explanation.

He was the one who decided when a relationship was over.

The buzzing in his ears resolved into a conversation that slowed as one face after another turned to him, eyes expectant. He blinked and tried to make sense of what De Laurentis said, aware of the other man's curiosity.

Ruthlessly Fabrizio sliced his gaze from hers and focused on the business at hand. If De Laurentis had any idea of using Jenna MacDonald to distract him, he was sorely mistaken. If anything, her presence incited a bloodlust for victory unlike any he'd known.

Fabrizio let his lips curve in a lethal smile and delivered his first salvo.

Fortunately he was the only one in the crowded room aware that he gave the crucial negotiations just half his attention. The other half lingered over plans for his faithless ex-lover.

The negotiations passed in a blur for Jenna.

Concentrating on the rapid-fire back and forth exchange was beyond her, despite her now excellent Italian. She refused to blush at the memory of how it came to be so good. To gain fluency in a language, they said you should take a native speaker as a lover.

Her throat closed over a shocking surge of hysterical laughter as she watched the man on the other side of the table effortlessly dominate the proceedings. She hadn't taken Fabrizio as a lover. He'd taken her.

One chance look across the crowded café in Saint Mark's Square.

One hour of conversation with a black-haired stranger over minuscule coffee cups and delicious sweet pastries. She'd been oblivious of tourists and pigeons and everything but the hot silver of his eyes and the approving curve of his thin, sculpted lips as he coaxed her into conversation.

One afternoon letting him guide her through *his* Venice, to secret places few tourists ever saw, from crumbling, ancient beauty to modern luxury, the taste of delicious seafood and the sensation of the sea breeze in her hair as they watched the sun set in a fiery glow.

One evening of fairy-tale perfection that had made her feel like Cinderella finding her prince. Except there'd been no running away at midnight. Instead there'd been a night of seduction, passion, bliss, unlike anything she'd ever known.

One night was all it had taken for her to lose her heart and put her career plans on hold now her internship at a plush Venetian hotel was over.

One night had led to another and another, until she was installed in Fabrizio Armati's Roman palazzo as his lover.

No, not his lover. He'd finally made that cruelly clear. His *mistress*. His disposable mistress, not good enough to claim a place in his rarefied world.

The pain of that rejection had cleaved her heart. Alone in the world, she'd poured everything of herself into their relationship, believing she'd found her soul mate.

Jenna blinked, trying to focus on the intense discussion around her rather than the slash of raw pain through her middle. She'd been primed for this meeting, though surprised at her inclusion among the corporate lawyers and strategists.

'It's agreed, then,' her boss, Luca De Laurentis, said. 'We'll meet again once the amendments are drafted. In the meantime I look forward to a personal inspection of the Florentine property before we sign.'

She breathed a sigh of relief, realising the negotiations hadn't required her input after all. Tension wound her so tight, she wasn't sure she'd have found her voice.

'As I look forward to viewing the Amalfi estate.' A flash of bright steel pinioned her as Fabrizio's eyes narrowed on her across the room. Immediately Jenna lifted her chin. He had no hold over her. If she told herself often enough, she might even come to believe it.

Chairs scraped back and everyone stood. Everyone except Fabrizio. Jenna yanked her gaze away, refusing to give in to temptation and watch him. She grabbed her briefcase and turned with her colleagues towards the door.

'One last thing.' That familiar voice cut like a honed blade through soft flesh. 'I have limited time available. I'll have a briefing on the Villa Bellini now before my site visit.'

'As you wish. Ms MacDonald can provide all the details you need.' Luca De Laurentis caught Jenna's eye and smiled. 'Jenna, come and see me in my office when you've finished with Signor Armati.'

Finished with Signor Armati.

Jenna gritted her teeth, wishing she had finished with him once and for all.

She pasted on a smile for Signor De Laurentis. 'Of course, sir.'

Slowly the room emptied. She was aware of Fabrizio indicating that his staff should go too. And still she couldn't bring herself to meet his eyes. It took all the willpower she had to stand her ground. Six months and still her heart wrenched at the sight of him.

Finally she mastered herself, placing her briefcase on the gleaming table. It snicked open and she pulled out her neat précis of the Villa's details as well as her tablet, ready to answer every question about the gracious old hotel.

When there was nothing else to distract her she took a deep breath and lifted her head, only to fall into that molten pewter stare that once had so effortlessly bewitched her.

Now it held no softness, just the threat of retribution.

Chapter Two

'THE VILLA BELLINI IS A remarkable old hotel, as I'm sure you're aware.' Jenna planted her damp palms on the table and spoke to a point just over Fabrizio's shoulder. 'It's maintained market share despite economic uncertainties that impacted on tourism performance elsewhere.'

Silence.

She paused and glanced down at her carefully prepared information. Not that she needed it. As relieving manager of the hotel, she knew this by heart.

'What, in particular, did you want to know about the Villa?'

Again that brooding silence. Was it imagination or did she really feel Fabrizio's gaze slide down from her face to her cleavage? Her breasts tingled and seemed to swell and she sucked in a furtive breath, willing herself not to react.

'We could start,' he said at last, his voice ringing in accusation, 'with why you ran from me like a thief in the night.'

Jenna's head jerked up. 'Hardly a thief.' She raised her brows, remembering the wardrobe of sexy, couture dresses she'd left behind, the jewelled sandals, dainty evening bags and slinky bikinis. Especially the bikinis. Fabrizio had enjoyed those so much.

Heat flared anew beneath her skin as her head filled with a memory of the pair of them entwined by the pool, Fabrizio deftly peeling away a bikini he'd bought her. It was made entirely of string and gilt beads.

He shrugged and she kept her face on his deep red tie rather than the rise and dip of those broad shoulders.

'You ran without a word.'

'I did not run!' She met his eyes and a jolt of adrenaline shot through her, tingling right to her soles in her black patent stiletto-heeled shoes. 'And I left you a note.'

'An email.' His mouth twisted in a sneer. 'What way is that to end a relationship?'

'Is that what you called it? A relationship? How cosy that sounds.' It was Jenna's turn to curl her lip. Ice frosted her blood as she recalled how he'd dismissed her and all they'd shared with such easy contempt. 'As far as I'm concerned, an email was entirely appropriate to end our *arrangement*.'

Fabrizio's eyes narrowed to slits but she refused to back down.

'An email that said nothing except that you'd decided to leave.' A pulse ticked in his jaw and Jenna felt a moment's triumph that she'd made Fabrizio Armati *feel* something. Even anger was a step up from simple sexual desire.

Jenna straightened, smoothing her clammy palms down her pencil skirt. His eyes followed the movement and she quickly grasped her hands behind her back, unnerved that he should knock her off balance so easily.

She'd spent the meeting with her gaze locked

on his arrogant, beautiful face, eagerly memorising details already imprinted on her brain. His heavy-lidded eyes that made her think of the sultry passion they'd shared. The groove at one corner of his mouth that deepened when he smiled. The tiny, jagged scar on his chin that he'd acquired in a childhood accident.

It was infuriating that even now she found herself eating him up with her eyes.

'What explanation do you have?' He lounged back in his leather chair, but his eyes were sharp as lasers. 'Why did you go like that?'

For a moment Jenna was tempted to blurt out everything. But that would serve no purpose. What she'd thought they'd shared hadn't been real. Besides, she refused to reveal how much his dismissal had hurt.

Hurt? That made it sound simple and complete. Finished. Instead it was a festering wound that still wouldn't heal.

'We'd been together for what? Seven months?' She shrugged and congratulated herself on her insouciance. He'd never realise she knew to the day how long they'd been together. 'The attraction had run its course. It was time for me to leave.'

Something flared in those deep-set eyes that almost made her step back from the table. But Jenna was through with letting Fabrizio Armati ride roughshod through her life. He mightn't like what she'd done but he'd coped. Only his pride was bruised.

'Now, did you have any specific questions about the Villa Bellini?' She made a show of shuffling the papers before her. 'Or was this a pretence to get me alone?'

'Why would I want to do that?' He steepled his hands under his chin. 'I've already known you *intimately*.' His softly spoken words had the lash of a whip. 'And the novelty has definitely worn off.'

Jenna felt blood sting her cheeks as she met his cool gaze. How dare he speak to her like that?

Yet it was only what she should have expected from someone so callous.

'My feelings precisely,' she said smoothly. 'I see I don't have to explain my reason for leaving after all.' She paused, watching his brows cram together in a thunderous frown. Expert lover that he was, she'd bet it was the first time a woman had claimed to tire of him. 'Why get stuck in a rut once boredom sets in?'

She made a show of packing up her papers, ignoring the bristling antagonism radiating from across the table. 'So if we've cleared that up, I'll be on my way. I have work to do.'

'So eager to run back to your current protector?'

Jenna froze, her nape prickling at the slimy implication in his words.

'Eager to get back to work. Coming to Rome for this meeting has taken a chunk of time out of my schedule.'

Fabrizio surged to his feet, his knuckles white on the conference table, his mouth twisting, almost as if with pain. Jenna stared, telling herself she was a fool to imagine vulnerability where there was none. Fabrizio was many things, but vulnerable wasn't one of them.

'And what's on that schedule? A little afternoon sex on De Laurentis's desk? Or shopping for titillating lingerie to amuse him tonight?'

Jenna gasped at the naked fury in those hard, silver eyes. And at the knot of pain high in her chest that stifled her breathing. It took a full thirty seconds for her to find her voice.

'*You* may not be capable of seeing a woman as anything other than a sex object, Fabrizio, but there are some men who appreciate our talents.'

His eyes shadowed in a way she'd never seen before. Something more than anger lurked there. For a disturbing second her brain tried to persuade her it was regret, even pain, until she realised that was wishful thinking.

'And which *talent* did you use to impress De Laurentis?' he snarled, leaning across the wide table till the space between them shrank alarmingly. 'Did you get down on your knees before him and—'

'That's enough!' The words were a crack of sound. Her chest heaved as she tried and failed to drag in air. Her ears buzzed with the heavy pulse of her racing blood. She thought she'd scraped rock bottom the day she left him, but she'd been wrong. This proof of his casual cruelty sliced straight to her heart all over again. Pain consumed her. How could she have imagined he might have regrets?

'Signor De Laurentis is my employer, and a very good one too. There is nothing sexual between us.'

'You ask me to believe that?' His jaw jutted belligerently.

'I don't give a damn what you believe, Fabrizio. But I've never lied to you.'

Not until today, when she pretended she'd grown bored with their relationship when the opposite was true. She'd fallen for Fabrizio hook, line and sinker all those months ago. His betrayal had all but torn her apart. All through the meeting she'd battled a resurgence of those tender feelings, only to have him turn on her with his vile accusation.

Somehow she had to banish what she'd once felt for him. Wretchedly she told herself he was doing a fine job of helping her.

Jenna speared Fabrizio with a look. 'He employed me because of my professional skills.'

'Skills such as industrial espionage? Is that how he managed to lever a better deal in this property swap? I should have known he'd stoop to any advantage he could get, even to hiring a woman whose value is in the insider information she gleaned in my bed.'

Jenna planted her hands on her hips and willed her howling outrage into silence. She was fast losing track of the number of ways Fabrizio insulted her. Enough was enough.

'What secrets would they be, Fabrizio? You never shared commercially sensitive information with me. In fact, as far as I recall, we never talked business, presumably because you assumed I wasn't capable of understanding anything as taxing as profits and losses.'

He stared back at her as if she'd grown two heads. As well he might. Never in their time together had they argued and, Jenna realised now, she'd been content to go along with Fabrizio's plans for the pair of them. She'd spent her time in a delicious haze of love, delighted at his thoughtfulness and passion. And he *had* been thoughtful – catering to her every whim and encouraging her delight in each new experience they shared.

How naïve she'd been. She'd never once noticed all that was wrong with their relationship until that last fateful day when the rose-coloured glasses had been dragged from her eyes and smashed underfoot.

'You never took more than a passing interest in the career I had before I met you.' She hadn't realised till she left him how much that rankled. 'Or my aspirations for the future.'

Aspirations for the future! How he'd laugh if he ever found out they'd once, briefly, centred on him.

'I didn't give your rival any trade secrets, Fabrizio, because you never trusted me with them!' Jenna slid her tablet into her briefcase and snapped it shut. 'Whatever agreement my boss negotiated with you, he did it without any input from me.'

On the contrary, if she'd had any say in the matter, which she didn't being so low in the De Laurentis hierarchy, she'd have begged he not consider a deal that included swapping the lovely old Villa Bellini for a parcel of prime real estate in Florence, currently owned by Fabrizio Armati. She had no illusions that Fabrizio would keep her on at the Villa once it was his. The savage gleam in his eyes told her he didn't know anything about letting bygones be bygones.

Jenna slid her briefcase from the table and turned to the door.

'Wait! We haven't finished.'

She shook her head. He may not have finished but she had. Jenna hung onto her composure by the merest thread. Any minute now and the welling pain she battled would swamp her, breaking down her resolve to appear in control.

She refused to let him reduce her to tears ever again.

'We've finished, Fabrizio. I don't ever need to see you again.' She drew a shuddering breath of relief that it was true. 'If you have any questions about the Villa, I'll answer via email.'

Jenna had taken three steps towards the door when he spoke.

'Weren't you paying attention earlier, *cara*?' He paused and foreboding skittered through her, freezing her spine. She didn't like the smug satisfaction in his tone. 'I intend to check out every corner of your precious Villa before I agree to proceed with this deal. That means I'll be staying there over the weekend.'

Again that pause. This time it lasted so long the hair rose on her nape. When he spoke again his tone was silky yet lethal. 'And you've been assigned the honour of conducting me on a personal tour.'

Chapter Three

'AS YOU CAN SEE, THE beach is completely private.' Fabrizio watched Jenna gesture towards the secluded cove of pristine sand between the headlands before turning briskly back to the path.

His ex-lover was nervous. From the moment he'd arrived she hadn't been still.

Did she have any idea how movement turned her prim dark suit from corporate camouflage to pure enticement? He doubted it. She wore a distant expression and kept twitching her collar together as if the conservatively cut business shirt was too revealing.

But following her through the manicured gardens to the sea, he'd been in a perfect position to appreciate the way her skirt clung to her taut backside and gently swelling hips with every step. She'd negotiated the stairs in her high-gloss heels, more suited to a trendy office in Rome, or drinks on a secluded city terrace before a long, friendly, shared siesta.

He dragged his mind back to the purpose of his visit.

Face it, Fabrizio, she *is* the reason for the visit.

One of his staff could have done the final check of the hotel. But from the moment he'd realised

Jenna MacDonald was working for De Laurentis, managing the place, there'd been no question but he'd take care of this himself.

Fabrizio didn't like unfinished business and Jenna MacDonald was precisely that.

He resented it. Before her his life had been so simple. Business was serious and women were for pleasure. That had always worked for him and it was the way he intended it to work in future. But she'd upset the neat balance of his life, invading his thoughts when he should have been concentrating on bringing off yet another commercial coup.

She swung round and for the first time their eyes met. Heat soldered his gut to his pelvis as that aquamarine stare drilled into him. It was the same enticing colour as the sea fringing the golden sand. How often had he lost himself in those liquid depths as he'd surrendered himself to ecstasy?

Possessiveness roared through him. No matter what she said, she hadn't finished with him. That surge of attraction wasn't dead. He saw it in her eyes, in the rapid pulse beating in her throat, in the flush washing over her collarbone.

So why had she run from him?

'Are you coming?' she challenged.

Fabrizio clamped his jaw on a description of exactly how he'd like to come, hard and fast inside her. She'd be gasping his name, those sexy heels locked behind him as he drove her to heaven, recanting her lie that she'd grown bored with him.

'Of course. I don't want to miss a moment.'

Her eyes narrowed suspiciously. 'Our clients enjoy it here as much for the seclusion as for the coast, but there's a spectacular view of the sea from every guest room.'

'So you can listen to the waves from your bed? I understand it's supposed to be very soothing.'

Her eyes widened. Obviously she remembered telling him that when he'd once taken her to Sorrento for the weekend. The closest they'd got to the sea was the balcony of their bedroom as they feasted on seafood and wine before abandoning the meal in favour of their bed.

Fabrizio swallowed a growl of protest at what she'd thrown away. As lovers they'd been spectacular together. Even out of bed, chatting easily, finding shared likes and dislikes, they'd been remarkably… compatible.

'As you say, Villa Bellini is the ultimate in luxury relaxation. It's an excellent investment.' She turned and began climbing the rock-cut steps up the cliff.

He stood back and enjoyed the view. His fingers prickled and his pulse revved at the temptation of that ripe peach bottom lovingly outlined with every step she took.

Fabrizio shook himself. He was here because he wanted answers.

And vengeance, though he was unsure what form that would take.

Now he realised all that could wait.

What he wanted most urgently was Jenna.

Fabrizio took the stairs three at a time, halting close behind her as she reached the cliff top, crowding her so she swung round, a gasp on her ruby lips. A few wisps of gold had escaped the hair she'd secured so neatly and her face was flushed with exertion. He smiled, imagining her panting for breath beneath him, her hips cradling him, her skin like silk against his.

She must have read his thoughts for suddenly she was retreating, almost stumbling back along the white gravel path as he stalked towards her.

She swallowed hard then seemed to gather herself. She stopped and stood straight, her hand going to her collar in that tell-tale gesture. Her chin lifted and her eyebrows arched as if challenging him.

Hadn't she realised yet he never ignored a challenge?

Fabrizio smiled slowly and watched her mouth tighten.

'Now that you've seen the grounds, and the security arrangements, I'll leave you in Guido's capable hands for the rest of the tour. I'm afraid I have—'

'Whatever other work you have, you can forget it.' He paused, letting that sink in. 'You're mine for the duration of this visit.'

Her gasp of outrage was loud and delightfully satisfying. Had she really thought she could wipe her hands of him as if he was some nobody?

'De Laurentis assured me you'd answer all my questions personally. And I have lots of questions.' Purposefully he stepped forward, almost brushing her shoulder as he passed. 'We'll start in the kitchens.'

It was dusk by the time they finished. Fabrizio had been meticulous in his attention to detail and relentless in his questioning.

It was only the second time Jenna had seen Fabrizio the billionaire hotelier, rather than Fabrizio the charming, charismatic lover. Despite herself, she was impressed.

Whatever his reasons for putting her through the torture of a day in his company, she was in no doubt how he'd transformed his already sizeable inheritance into a commercial empire of luxury hotels. She'd always known him to be quick-witted and intelligent, but hours answering his probing questions left her both exhausted and admiring. His interest in every aspect of the business, and the way his thoughts galloped ahead to potential opportunities and problems were impressive. Her goal was one day to run a hotel of her own and in other circumstances it would have been wonderful to work for him.

If it weren't for the history between them.

She pushed open the double doors to the royal suite. The spacious foyer led into a grand salon, decorated in muted greens and golds, reflecting the colours of the gardens, sea and sandy beach visible through the open French doors.

He walked past her, taking in with a sweeping glance the priceless antiques and meticulous per-fection of the delicate silk hangings and fine art.

Carefully she shut the door to the hallway and crossed the lovingly polished wood floor. Another five minutes to show him his suite and she'd be free. She sighed, imagining half an hour in a scented bath, sipping a glass of her favourite Frascati.

'I applaud your attention to detail.' He'd stopped to investigate the bottle of wine nestling in the silver wine cooler. Beside it was an artistically arranged platter of summer fruit and a selection of wafer-thin almond and citrus biscotti. 'No grapes, I notice.'

'You only enjoy grapes as a source of wine.' Jenna shrugged. 'Why serve what I know you don't like?' She made no apology for providing his favourite wine either.

'Using your inside information about me?' His expression wasn't accusing, just curious.

'Why not? I'm sure you'd do the same. Besides, it's my job to ensure your stay here is a success.'

Because then he'd acquire the hotel from Luca De Laurentis. She repressed a sigh. Once Fabrizio owned the place, she'd be out of a job and the one she'd been offered by Luca, while fantastic on paper, was far from the sort of work she dreamed of. A promotion to a huge city hotel would be challenging and a step up the career ladder, but Jenna preferred the challenges of delivering high-quality service in a smaller, more intimate hotel.

'You're young to manage this.' A wide gesture encompassed the estate.

Jenna smoothed her hand down her jacket and busied herself turning on lamps. 'Twenty-eight isn't so young. And I'm the relieving manager. The permanent manager is on sick leave.'

But Fabrizio was right. The chance to take on responsibility for this jewel of a hotel had been a thrilling, if initially daunting responsibility. She adored it. This was exactly the sort of work at which she excelled.

'Let me show you your suite.'

'I thought you'd never offer.'

Stoically Jenna ignored his murmured jibe and led the way through a private dining area to the vast master bedroom.

It hit her as she paused in the doorway that the

decorator might have had Fabrizio in mind when designing this space. With a more modern yet no less deluxe atmosphere, the room blended silvery pewter and charcoal shades. The dying light and billowing sheer curtains created a softness that contrasted with its clean lines. A spotlight illuminated an exquisite antique stone carving of a horse, almost but not quite drawing the eye from the vast bed.

Jenna's breath clogged in her throat as she felt him come up behind her, close enough for his heat to warm her. And still she had trouble dragging her eyes from that silvery bedspread.

Her knees were unsteady as she marched across the room, collecting a remote control to open wide the curtains.

She was tired, that's all, after a day confined with the one man who'd always been able to make her weak-kneed. He hadn't lost that ability, even when he'd lost her respect. Jenna castigated herself for still being affected by him. Even the sound of his deep, dark chocolate voice was a secret delight when he wasn't throwing jibes her way.

'And here's the bathroom.' She put down the remote and stepped into the room of travertine marble and glass. The view of the sea from the sunken bath was perfection and no expense had been spared. She gestured to a collection of crystal jars. 'The bath salts are labelled.'

Not that Fabrizio would bother. He was a shower man, only soaking in a tub when sharing.

Fire washed her breasts and throat at the unwanted memory and she spun around, only to find herself impaled by hot silver eyes. His stare sent a shiver of erotic heat rippling from her nipples to her womb as easily as if he'd flicked a switch.

She knew that look. How well she knew it!

And her body's response.

Jenna blinked and stepped back instinctively, horrified and ashamed at how longing instantly slammed into her. She came up against the cool marble countertop, hands clutching the hard surface.

Fabrizio moved further into the room, his gaze never wavering. She swallowed a lump of panic and cleared her throat.

'Would you like to see the rest of the suite now?' Her voice was too throaty, like an invitation. She swallowed again.

'Why bother? One bed is enough.' His voice dipped low.

Enough for what? He wasn't talking about sleep, not with that predatory gleam in his eyes.

The atmosphere between them sparked with static energy that sucked the oxygen from the air. Her body grew heavy as the pulse of her blood turned sluggish and expectant.

Jenna shook her head, her eyes never leaving his as he came to a halt well inside her personal space.

'If you don't want to see any more, I'll leave you to relax and explore at your leisure.' Her voice was clipped and cool. If you ignored its husky edge. 'Will you dine here or downstairs?'

'I'm not ready to relax. I find myself…restless.' His mouth curved in a smile as sharp as a tiger's. 'And it's not dinner I'm hungry for.'

He lifted a hand as if to brush her cheek and her head reared back, indignation exploding at his innuendo.

'You really think you can just walk in here and have…' Jenna shook her head, unable to say the words.

'Have *you*?' His smile widened. 'Oh, yes.'

Outrage poured through her, drenching the betraying spark of arousal she'd felt from the moment he'd got close.

'You have the most colossal ego.' She straightened, her hands fisting at her sides as she fought not to lash out. 'I'll leave the two of you alone to enjoy the company.' She stepped forward, turning her shoulder as she brushed past him.

There was a bark of laughter, abrupt and surprisingly appealing, then strong fingers clamped around her wrist.

'Not so fast.'

She stopped, heart thumping, and stared down to where his hard, olive-skinned fingers shackled her hand. Six whole months since he'd touched her, a fleeting kiss at her throat before he left her in the cool of dawn, and still he had the power to undo her. If she let him.

Jenna shivered, control hanging by a thread. 'Let. Me. Go.'

'You must be joking.' Her gaze wrenched up to snare on his. 'Now that I've finally found you I won't let you go so easily.'

Chapter Four

'FINALLY FOUND ME?' JENNA SHOOK her head so violently wisps of hair feathered around her cheeks. 'That implies you missed me, which is impossible since by definition a mistress is disposable and replaceable.'

She kept her expression shuttered. Not by so much as a flicker of reaction would she let him guess how much the word *mistress* hurt. How hearing Fabrizio describe her like that, so dismissively, had curdled the secret hope she'd once nurtured.

His eyes narrowed and she felt his scrutiny like a blade scraping sensitive skin. She jerked her arm back but couldn't break his hold.

'It also implies you looked for me.' Her mouth twisted with sour humour. 'Which, again, we both know you're far too busy to do. So don't play games with me, Fabrizio.'

If she'd expected to see a spark of shame or regret she'd have been disappointed. Just as well she'd come to accept that her ex-lover would never feel anything so honest for her.

He looked more furious than ever. Despite his passionate nature, Fabrizio's brand of anger was of the ice-cold variety. His face turned stony, his jaw set in a grim line that would have looked right at home on some ancient Roman gladiator. Those pale eyes were like shards of ice as they raked her.

'Oh, I looked, *cara*.' His nostrils flared as he took a deep breath. 'I scoured Rome for you. Have you any idea how dangerous the city can be for a woman alone? And at that time?' He gave her hand a little shake. 'When they told me you'd left the palazzo before it was even properly light! *Per la Madonna!*'

Jenna's eyes bulged. 'You're not serious.'

Never had it crossed her mind he'd search for her.

No. It was impossible.

His head thrust close, his breath hot on her face. 'Never more serious. What did you expect? You suddenly disappear, leaving most of your things behind. You slip out before the household is awake without arranging a driver or even a taxi.'

She started and he nodded. 'Oh, yes. I checked. My staff contacted every taxi and car hire company in Rome and for a hundred kilometres beyond. I dealt with the hospitals personally.'

Jenna stared, unable to match such actions, and the stark emotion in his voice and face, with the callous man she'd left behind. That man hadn't truly cared for her.

Yet Fabrizio said he'd checked to see if she was injured? Personally checked?

'Nothing to say?' His mouth was a thin, uncompromising line.

'There was no need for that.' Her voice was raspy with shock. 'I'm perfectly capable of looking after myself.'

His eyebrows soared. 'And when the only witness to your departure said you looked like death?

That you stumbled just getting out the door and he thought you'd had some sort of shock?' His head reared back and he surveyed her down that splendid, aristocratic nose. 'For all I knew, you'd collapsed in a gutter somewhere, or were preyed on by some street gang.'

Jenna pressed the heel of her hand to her thumping heart, trying to take in the enormity of what Fabrizio had revealed.

He'd searched, actually combed Rome for her?

She felt light-headed, trying to grapple with such a foreign concept. It didn't make sense. None of it did.

'But why? Why go to so much bother?' Wonderingly she met his gaze and caught a flash of something unfamiliar in those dark pewter depths.

'Why?' His lips twisted cruelly on the word. 'You have to ask why?' He shook his head, staring down at her as if he'd never seen her before.

A sudden jerk of his arm tugged her off balance. She fell against him, breast against hard, male heat, her hand splayed over superfine wool and powerful muscle.

'Because of this.' His head swooped down like a bird of prey on its target. The action was so swift she just had time to register shock before his mouth crashed into hers, forcing her head back. He gathered her in, one broad hand cradling the back of her skull. Dimly she realised he surrounded her, his legs planted around hers, shoulders blotting out the evening light, his body, his hands and mouth all she could feel.

Joy rose. Scalding, sudden, incandescent joy, at being within Fabrizio's embrace again.

Her body reacted instinctively, her lips parting hungrily under the pressure of his, her body softening against his taut frame. Her hand crept up to plunge in the crisp hair at the back of his head.

Yet somewhere amidst the overload of sensation, her brain tried to assert itself.

'No,' she gasped against his mouth. 'I don't—'

'But you do, don't you, *tesoro*?' His whispered, fervent words tracked a line across her cheek, to her ear and down her throat, making her shudder and her nipples peak with erotic pleasure. 'You do want this. You want *me*, just as I want you. It's always been like that between us. You can't hide it.'

She was melting, the core of her liquefying under the double assault of his words and his magic touch. Any minute now and her legs would give way completely. She grabbed his shoulders and hung on.

'Jenna!' His voice was sharp and demanding, dragging her heavy eyes open. 'You want me, don't you?'

He looked so fierce, so war-like, her insides gave a little quiver of fear, even though she knew he'd never physically hurt her. He looked like a man goaded almost beyond the limit of his control.

She shook her head, dazed by the impressions bombarding her, and his hold tightened. He crushed her against him.

'Say it, Jenna.' His lips found the secret place below and behind her ear and she shuddered with need. A moment later she caught the sound of fabric tearing and his hand was on her breast, hot and delicious through the fragile lace of her bra. 'Say it.'

Lust and longing. Curiosity and almost…fear

at his harsh expression. That wasn't anger or simple lust in those crystalline depths but something unfamiliar.

She thought of him searching for her, worrying for her, and her anger melted. Recklessness fired her blood at the realisation this would probably be the last time she felt this vibrant passion. With a sigh of defeat, she gave in to the inevitable.

She'd run from him but she'd never truly escaped.

Fisting her hands in his hair, Jenna pulled his head down and nipped him on the earlobe. His start of reaction was like a bolt of lightning zapping through all her erogenous zones. Always it had been like that. His pleasure was hers.

'I want you, Fabrizio.' The words emerged strong and true. 'Just like you want me.'

Lord help her. Would she ever be free of this spell he wove around her? Fear rose to choking point for the truth was she didn't want to be free. She loved him. Had loved him since that first day.

A sob rose in her throat and her eyes brimmed with burning self-anger.

Then Fabrizio's hand pushed under her bra to fondle her breast and her despair was lost in a surge of furious desire. Her teeth found his neck and she nipped hard just at the curve to his shoulder.

He gasped, and an instant later his hands were at her waist, hoisting her up onto the bed hard marble counter. A tearing tug at her shirt, an expert flick of his hand at the front catch of her bra and her breasts swung free.

Jenna's eyes lost focus, her lids lowering as he bent and suckled hard at her breast. Pleasure twanged like a fine wire of arousal stretching from her breast to the juncture of her thighs and she shuddered with delight. It was at once familiar and yet new, as if this encounter she'd never expected delved into uncharted territory. Greedily she grabbed his dark head and held it to her breast as she arched into him, her head lolling against the wall mirror.

How she'd missed this – the pleasure he gave her so readily, so easily. More, she'd missed *him*, the man who, even now, consumed her thoughts, her very soul.

Dimly she registered other things, the slap of his leather belt against her thigh as he wrenched at his trousers, the tearing of a condom wrapper. She shuffled closer to the edge of the vanity unit, needy for him. So needy her skin felt too tight for her body.

'Yes,' he groaned approvingly. 'Like that.'

Large hands clamped her thighs and hauled her right to the edge of the counter, then tunnelled up under her skirt, pushing it higher and higher.

'You still wear stockings.'

Was that relief in his voice as he palmed her bare upper thighs? She couldn't tell over the rocketing pound of her pulse, but the gleam in his eyes was pure masculine appreciation.

At least that was something he'd never stinted to give her. Maybe that's why she'd made the fatal error of falling in love with him. Fabrizio was charming, effortlessly charismatic and passionate. Yet he had never returned her love.

Desperate heat glazed her eyes and she blinked.

He looked up, frowning. An instant later his hand was cradling her cheek as he took her mouth in a lush, open-mouthed kiss that was tender and sexy and pure bliss.

Jenna's heart tore wide open, the tightness in her chest easing as light and heat filled her. She cupped his face, tilting her head and allowing all her confused emotions to surface as she gave him kiss for kiss.

She hadn't felt whole since she'd left him. But this, now, felt so right.

His hands were still on her face as he pulled back, his breath a soft brush of air on her cheeks, the tangy scent of his skin so familiar and enticing.

For a moment she was sure he was about to speak. Then his lips firmed and she felt movement between her thighs. Her silk panties were dragged aside and in one long, easy movement Fabrizio filled her, pulling her to him so hard it felt as if he reached the very heart of her. Or maybe that was because of the way his silvery gaze held her, refusing to let her go.

How had she forgotten this exquisite perfection? This feeling that the world had stopped spinning and nothing existed but the pair of them, as near to one being as it was possible for a couple to be.

Jenna tried to fill her lungs but her chest was too tight to expand properly. She felt light-headed, drowning in the glow of wellbeing that encompassed her when Fabrizio held her like this, looked at her like this.

For a moment she could almost convince herself this was more than sex, that he felt—

She shut her eyes, blocking out that gleaming gaze, knowing she should be done with that fantasy. But he didn't let her withdraw. His lips tasted hers, softly, temptingly, as his fingertips brushed whorls of pleasure from the tips of her breasts to her ribs.

The sweet magic of it made her moan, her eyes flickering open.

Instantly she was snared by his expression, a frown of concentration vying with the triumph in his smile and a look she wanted to think was tenderness in his eyes.

When he moved, taking up a primitive, urgent rhythm that matched the frantic pulse of her blood, she couldn't look away. Even when the ripples of excitement became a tsunami of pleasure, rolling in waves, shaking them like flotsam on a stormy sea, they rode the maelstrom together till on one impossibly high crest of pleasure they both shattered and sank.

Chapter Five

THROUGH SLITTED EYES, JENNA WATCHED the dawn light steal into the room. Beyond the balcony the sea was a fathomless grey. Rather like the thoughts swirling in her head.

Her pulse hammered a too-fast tattoo as her sated body gradually slumped back to earth. The rapture of Fabrizio's lovemaking still wrapped around her, luxurious and decadently sensual. Yet as the bliss faded, bleak thoughts beat at her consciousness.

'What are you thinking?' The low rumble of Fabrizio's voice came from beneath her ear as she lay, abandoned, across his chest. Hot, satiny skin and the tickle of chest hair teased her.

She'd tried so often to resist the temptation of him yet her body, or perhaps it was her heart, continually undermined her resolve. Each time she wondered if this was the last time they'd be together and had been unable to turn away.

She should turn her back on him if she wanted to keep her sanity. He'd come close to destroying her once already.

Did it make it better or worse that she knew he'd never reciprocate her feelings? For him this was only skin-deep.

'Jenna?' That clipped word sounded sharp.

'I'm thinking it's time I got up and went to my

own quarters.'

One night had turned into three as Fabrizio extended his stay at the villa and Jenna, horrifyingly weak-willed, had spent every one in his suite.

'Why is it so important no-one finds out we've spent the night together?' His tone turned belligerent and she almost smiled in gratitude. An angry Fabrizio was far easier to resist than one intent on seduction.

She opened her mouth to answer him then stopped. He didn't need to hear about her increasingly desperate need to assert some independence from him and all he made her feel. Let him think this was all about keeping their liaison secret from her colleagues.

'This is my workplace, Fabrizio. These are my colleagues.' Though not for long once he took possession and she moved on to another post in the De Laurentis hotel empire. 'I prefer to keep my personal and business lives separate.'

'You're too sensitive,' he growled, which was his way of saying her work didn't matter.

She levered herself up off his torso and made to slide away when long arms hauled her back. With a puff of exhaled air, she landed on top of him.

'No need to rush away. You've still got time.' His hand stroked possessively up and down her spine and she wondered if it was because she'd left him, and now managed to keep a sliver of independence from his wishes, that he wanted her so much.

Before, she'd been expendable.

As if sensing her sudden tension, he planted a gentle kiss on her forehead, then another, and something about the gesture loosened the knot in her belly. Fiercely she reminded herself it wasn't real tenderness, but that didn't stop her foolish heart racing.

'You still haven't told me why you walked out on me.' His dark velvet voice brushed tantalisingly across her flesh.

For three nights they'd avoided discussing the past, living only the present. Jenna was torn, knowing and hating the weakness that had kept her silent. She'd deliberately refused to contemplate all the problems between them just so she could spin out a little longer her time with him.

'You haven't told me why you checked out the taxis and hire cars, looking for me.' Hospitals she could understand – if he'd genuinely been worried for her wellbeing, but why the taxis?

He sighed and slid his hand to her bare thigh, circling one fingertip till she squirmed and snuggled closer.

'The airlines too.'

Shocked, she stilled. He'd checked the *flights* as well? 'Are they allowed to give out personal information about passengers?'

She felt his shoulders rise in a typical shrug. 'Where there's a will…'

Especially when the person enquiring was one of Italy's wealthiest men. Fabrizio wouldn't have baulked at using his influence to get the information he wanted. The reminder of his phenomenal power made her skin chill and prickle even though she lay against his hot body.

'You tried to make sure I'd left Italy?'

Jenna pushed herself up onto her arms so she could look down at him. She recognised that closed expression. Fabrizio was shutting her out. Why? What did he have to hide?

'What else did you do, Fabrizio?'

When he met her eyes, she saw a flash of anger and was shocked by its intensity. She shouldn't be. For days he'd repressed the fury she'd seen at that boardroom meeting. Fabrizio had fixed her with a stare that should have incinerated her where she sat. Yet he'd never delivered on the searing threat in his eyes. Here at Villa Bellini he'd kept his temper in check.

Jenna met his glare and refused to back down. How could he hurt her any more than he had already?

'What else, Fabrizio?' She wasn't going to let this go.

'I had enquiries made in your home town. To see if you'd returned.'

Slowly Jenna straightened. 'You had people search for me in Britain?' She felt her eyes widen. Why? He hadn't wanted her enough to introduce her to his precious family or consider making her a permanent part of his life, yet he'd searched for her across Europe? What had that cost him? More to the point, she couldn't imagine the proud, self-contained man she knew doing that.

She shuffled to the edge of the bed, planting her feet on the luxurious carpet, as if grounding herself in reality.

'I can't believe you did that.'

His actions scared her.

For days she'd let herself pretend the past and the future didn't matter. That they had this moment out of time. Now she was forced to face reality.

Who Fabrizio was, how powerful. How unequal they were.

Jenna was alone in the world, trying to build a career in the foreign country she'd fallen in love with. She'd made the appalling mistake of believing herself Cinderella to Fabrizio's Prince Charming. He was a billionaire tycoon from an aristocratic Italian family who saw her as nothing more than light entertainment. Yet he had the wealth and power to set his minions on a fruitless search for her across Rome and far beyond.

For the first time ever, Jenna felt completely powerless beside him. She had no-one but herself to rely on, no fond relatives to support her. Fabrizio had his powerful family and all the resources money could buy.

In one swift movement she was off the bed, sweeping up a discarded wrap and hauling it on as she stumbled across the room, putting as much distance as she could between herself and Fabrizio.

'What do you want from me?' she whispered, crossing her arms tight across her body and staring out at the dark sea.

'Revenge.' His voice came from right behind her and she spun round to see him naked and imposing, standing within touching distance. For once it wasn't his superb masculinity that caught her attention, but the fire in his eyes. 'I wanted to make you pay for leaving like that. When we met again, I wanted to make your life hell.'

Jenna tasted the rusty tang of blood in her mouth as she bit her lip. Fear and distress tore at her. She shrank back but he simply followed, stepping closer till she was crammed up against the cool glass of the French door to the balcony.

'But I've changed my mind,' he said finally. She followed the movement of muscles in his broad throat as he swallowed. 'I want you back. I want you with me.'

Jenna shook her head, struggling to take it in. How often had she dreamed of Fabrizio coming after her and begging her to return? It was a foolish dream but she'd never been able to shake its secret allure.

In her dreams he came because he realised he loved her. As if! He hadn't grown to love her in the months they'd been together, so fury and a desire for revenge certainly wouldn't do it. Nor would three nights in his bed.

He *wanted* her. He didn't need or love her.

'No. That's not possible.'

But it is, the voice of temptation whispered. *You want it too.*

'Of course it's possible. Haven't we just proved that?' One sable eyebrow arched knowingly as he swept an arm towards the rumpled bed they'd shared. Satisfaction lurked in the grooves curling at the edges of his mouth, and in his polished pewter eyes.

'Nevertheless, it's not going to happen.'

Fabrizio's face hardened, his smile flattening into a grim line, the light in his eyes changing to something harsh.

'If you think I'm going to let you go now, Jenna, you don't know me at all.'

She straightened her shoulders, pulling the slippery silk tie of her robe into a tight bow at her waist, wishing she had something more substantial than a wrap to protect her from his stark determination.

'You don't have a choice,' she murmured huskily, surprised to find her larynx half paralysed. 'You can't force me to stay with you.'

She had to remind herself they had no future despite the unsated longing between them. Dully she recognised that for her part it would never be eradicated. This man was in her blood.

His eyes narrowed and fear brushed her flesh again at the feral possessiveness in his expression. He looked dangerous. Half tamed. Like some renegade, not an urbane city businessman.

Her breath stalled as panic clutched her.

Or was it excitement? Fabrizio's look of primitive ownership sent a thrill through her that shattered every indignant denial hovering on her lips.

To be so wanted by him, to be claimed by him, spoke to her at some deep, primal level.

What would he do to keep her? How far would he go?

He took one step closer, brushing up against her breasts. They tingled, sending a current of electricity jolting straight to her pelvis.

She drew in a sharp breath, inhaling the spicy scent of his skin and her head swam. Behind her the cold glass seemed the only reminder of the world beyond her and Fabrizio.

'But I won't need to force you. You'll stay because you want to. Won't you, Jenna?' His mouth curved in a slow, devastating smile that made her heart loop the loop. 'You don't really want to leave me. I can see it in your gorgeous eyes. You want me as much as I want you.'

Jenna wanted to slap him down, reject his words and puncture his cocky certainty. She wanted him to leave her alone instead of muscling into her personal space, into the life she was trying to rebuild.

But she couldn't. Her slow exhale tasted of defeat.

He was right. Despite the pain, the lack of trust, the unevenness of what they felt for each other, part of her still clung to him. It was impossible to walk out on him a second time. She just didn't have it in her.

The realisation took her out at the knees and she slumped, despair stirring. His arms shot out, hard fingers grabbing her elbows and supporting her.

'Is it so very bad?' His terse question surprised her and she looked up. Yet she couldn't read his enigmatic expression. It was neither triumph nor anger, yet its intensity was like a brand on her skin. 'Being together has its benefits, hasn't it?'

He was asking? She was so used to Fabrizio asserting, it was disconcerting hearing him voice the question. Almost as if he was on shaky ground.

'For you.'

'And for you, *cara*. Don't try to pretend you don't enjoy what we share.' His head dipped towards hers and fear rose. Fear that she'd simply give in to the dictates of her body and his expert seduction.

With a surge of energy she pushed at his chest, holding him off till he pulled back, his frown questioning.

Jenna took advantage of the momentary respite to break out of his hold and sidle away to the other side of the open French door. She looked back at him across the opening.

Dawn light painted his skin golden, highlighting

the curves and planes of his muscled frame. His potent masculinity caught her breath, but it was the gleam in his clear gaze that twisted her heart. She loved his quick mind, his wit, his charm, his tender generosity even more than his perfect male body.

She sighed. She was doomed never to have the whole package that was Fabrizio Armati. He offered her physical pleasure, but nothing else.

She'd tried running and it hadn't worked. Now she'd found her way back into his bed she couldn't willingly leave it.

Yet perhaps she could protect herself. If she took a leaf out of his book. If she kept sex separate to the rest of her life. If she embarked on a liaison that was physical, pure pleasure, instead of emotional.

Impossible, screamed an inner voice. *You're already in love with him.*

What choice did she have? Retreat wasn't an option. All she could do was shore up her defences, barricade her heart as best she could and hope that intimacy, coupled with the knowledge Fabrizio would never return her feelings, might eventually kill those feelings for him.

Her shoulders slumped. 'You win, Fabrizio.'

She watched him struggle not to grin but the triumph was clear in his eyes as he closed the gap between them. He came up against her out-stretched palm.

'I'll be with you,' she said, her voice rough. 'But on my terms.'

Chapter Six

FABRIZIO SAT BACK IN HIS chair and let the discreet buzz of Rome's most chic and expensive restaurant wash over him.

He should be pleased with life. He'd closed the deal with De Laurentis on the terms he wanted and was now the possessor of the exquisite Villa Bellini. The land he wanted to purchase in the Seychelles was in the bag and negotiations in Hong Kong were going well. Closer to home he had Jenna, luscious, sexy Jenna back in his bed.

He watched the sway of her pert backside in that tight red dress as she sashayed through the dinner crowd to the ladies restroom.

He leaned back, wondering why he felt no satisfaction when everything was going as he wished.

Everything except his plans for Jenna.

For three weeks they'd been lovers again and she was just as amorous, just as bewitching as ever. In fact there was an edge to her passion that almost stole his breath, an intensity he was sure hadn't been there before. At first it had thrilled him. Now…

His skin prickled with the feeling that someone walked over his grave. He had an uneasy suspicion it didn't bode well.

She was back in his bed but that was all. Every day she insisted on leaving at dawn to go back to her tiny rented apartment across Rome to get ready for work. There were days when they couldn't meet for lunch because she claimed to be too busy at the office, though she no longer ran the Villa Bellini and was merely working in De Laurentis's Rome offices.

The thought of her working for his rival made his blood boil but she refused to stop. Even when he offered her the equivalent of a handsome wage, just so she could give up her job and be with him. Didn't she realise he'd look after her?

There were even nights when she was too busy or too tired to meet him. As if she had trouble fitting him in her schedule!

Worse, he read the smudged shadows under her bright eyes and wondered if he'd put them there.

Impossible! The sex was as stupendous as ever. Jenna wanted him as much as he did her. He was sure of it.

Yet he wasn't sure of her.

Why keep her distance? Why not simply move in with him? The hell of it was, the more she kept a space between them, the more he wanted to smash down the barriers she'd put up and keep her glued to his side, where she belonged.

He still hadn't got to the bottom of why she'd left him before. Every time he pressed she shied away and, wary of disrupting what they had, he backed off. But not knowing was like a sliver of ice jammed in his spine, keeping him on edge. He hated not knowing. It made him feel…not in control.

Jenna emerged back in the dining room and with a familiar swirl of excitement in his belly he watched her progress. Male heads turned as she passed but she seemed not to notice. Her eyes were on him and he felt a thrill of possessiveness. Those lush lips were glossy and full and soon they'd be on his.

He wouldn't take no for an answer tonight. For two days she'd claimed she hadn't the time to meet him. Tonight he'd remind her exactly what she'd been missing. She'd be putty in his hands. He couldn't wait.

'Ready to go? I've paid the bill.'

She paused, eyes widening a fraction. Then understanding dawned. He saw the moment her eyes turned smoky with anticipation and his heartbeat sped up. 'If you are.'

He was on his feet in a moment. With Jenna he was always ready. He'd never known such insistent, all-encompassing desire as for this woman.

Arm in arm they left the restaurant for his limo. Twenty minutes later they were in his palazzo.

'A drink?'

Jenna looked up into Fabrizio's handsome face and almost walked straight into his arms. She knew he'd sweep her up the grand marble staircase straight to his bedroom if she let him, that his question was mere politeness.

But she made herself nod. 'That would be lovely, thanks.'

She ignored the flash of surprise in his eyes and followed him into the vast, opulent salon where generations of Armatis had relaxed and entertained.

From his expression he'd obviously expected to have her in his bed in sixty seconds flat. As he usually did.

That was what frightened her, and made her delay. She'd thought by setting some boundaries, not moving in with him or being always at his beck and call, she could take the edge off this passion. But the strength of her feelings for Fabrizio hadn't faded.

What had she expected? That she could conquer love with a little distance?

Jenna squeezed her eyes shut, knowing she'd been a fool. She should never have let him persuade her back into his bed and his life. Every moment she spent with him just reinforced what she felt for him. She was in too deep. Extricating herself would take all her strength.

'Jenna? Are you all right?'

She snapped her eyes open and nodded. 'Of course. Just a little tired.' She nodded at the bottle in his hands. She knew from the label it was the premier wine made at his own vineyard. 'What are we celebrating?'

He glanced at the bottle of Prosecco then at her. 'Do I need an excuse when I have the pleasure of your company, *cara*?' His gaze drifted over her tight red dress, lingering on her cleavage, making her nipples harden. Fabrizio smiled wolfishly, deftly twisting the bottle till the cork came out with a pop.

Jenna's insides liquefied at the desire in his eyes. The same desire pounded in her bloodstream.

Yet part of her bridled that he took for granted she was there for his pleasure. It was true. She couldn't deny him when he took her in his arms. But that didn't make her feel any better about it, trapped as she was between her feelings for him and the cold, hard truth that the longer she stayed with Fabrizio, the more difficult their inevitable parting.

Finally he looked away and she almost sagged in relief.

He poured the sparkling wine into elegant crystal flutes. 'To us,' he said as he held out a glass to her and raised the other in salute.

Now. Now was the time to tell him.

'There may not be an us for much longer,' she said finally over the tightness in her throat. It was stupid of her. This was the chance she needed to break the web that bound her to him. Yet she'd hesitated because in her heart of hearts she needed him even though he didn't need her. Jenna pushed her shoulders back and stood straighter.

He froze, the glass at his lips, his brow furrowing in a dark scowl. 'What do you mean?'

Jenna sipped her wine, cool and delicious on her dry throat. 'I lost my job at the Villa Bellini when you acquired it. Now I'm being moved to another hotel, in Milan.'

'Milan!' Fabrizio's eyebrows disappeared into the black hair flopping over his brow. 'You're joking.'

'No joke, Fabrizio, it's my job. And a good one too. Signor De Laurentis is pleased with my work and this is a great opportunity.'

It was true, this would broaden her skills and look terrific on her résumé.

She didn't mention how torn she felt about leaving Fabrizio. She had no illusions that he'd come to Milan with her. He was Roman born and bred. Apart from the impossibility of him leaving his business, he'd stated more than once that living outside the capital was unbearable for more than a weekend retreat.

'It won't be forever. I don't want to work long term in a big hotel where everyone is that bit more anonymous. I prefer the smaller, exclusive venues, like Villa Bellini, where it's all about personalised service and a unique experience.' That was where her dream lay. One day she aimed to run her own hotel.

'Give up the job.' He snapped his fingers. 'You don't need it. Haven't I offered more than once to support you?'

The liquid heat in her belly solidified, curdling into bitterness.

'I won't take your money and live off you, Fabrizio.'

His frown became a glower but she merely tilted her chin higher. He might have an ancient lineage and pots of money but she had her pride.

'I only want to help.'

'You want me available.'

'*Basta!*' His glass slammed down on a table, bright droplets spilling to the floor. 'You're being deliberately difficult.'

Jenna walked to the ornate fireplace and put down her glass. With her damp hands, she might just drop the priceless crystal.

'It doesn't matter, Fabrizio. It's academic. I'm not giving up my career to become your live-in lover. My work is too important to me.'

'You're so obstinate!' He stalked towards her.

'And you're single-minded.' She jammed her hands on her hips, refusing to be intimidated as he stopped close enough to loom over her.

She'd given up her life for him once and look what it had got her – nothing except hurt and shame.

His eyes narrowed to a calculating scrutiny. Then, slowly, he smiled and her foolish heart tumbled.

'It's just as well I have the answer. There's an opening in one of my own hotels that would be perfect for you. In Rome. Not far from here.' His gesture took in the grand salon and the rest of his luxurious home.

He looked so like a cat eyeing a tasty bowl of cream that Jenna regarded him cautiously.

'When did this happen?'

'Recently. Very recently, which is why I didn't mention it before.'

'And what is the position?'

His shoulders rose in an easy shrug. 'It's a management role.'

'Manager? Assistant Manager?' When he didn't immediately respond she continued, 'Functions Manager? What?'

Fabrizio's mouth compressed. 'You can hear all about it when you report for work. My staff will fill you in.'

Jenna would bet her bottom dollar his staff knew nothing about any such vacancy. If he'd had a position for her he'd have mentioned it earlier. She knew he hated the fact she worked for Luca De Laurentis, even if Fabrizio no longer believed she spied for him.

'How do you know I can do it?'

'Sorry?' He stiffened.

'How do you know I have the appropriate qualifications?'

Fabrizio spread his hands, palms out. 'You ran the Villa Bellini, didn't you?'

'For a short time only. But you've never so much as seen my résumé.' He knew she'd worked in hotels, and that she'd come to Italy for an internship at a hotel in Venice that had finished the day before they'd met. Yet, Fabrizio had never questioned her qualifications. He'd never been that interested in her professional skills.

That knowledge jabbed a rod of steel through her spine.

'There is no job, is there?'

He waved his hand. 'Of course there is. I'm the CEO. If I want you to work in my hotel, you'll work there.'

Jenna shook her head. 'What about the staff who are already there? How will they feel about having me come in over the top of them? Especially to a job that's been created just for me?'

He didn't deny it. Jenna put out her hand to the mantelpiece and clung tightly as an invisible blow weakened her knees.

Part of her had actually hoped his offer was genuine. That he respected her enough to have her work in a real job because she was good at what she did.

She swallowed hard as bile rose in her throat. It was no use pretending. This could lead nowhere. Her relationship with Fabrizio was a dead end. She'd known it all along but hadn't been able to cut herself loose from him.

It was past time she set herself free.

'You can't see past your own convenience, can you? That's all that matters to you, Fabrizio. Making the world suit you.' Jenna drew a fortifying breath.

'Unfair!' His hand slashed through the air. 'We're amazing together. Don't lie and tell me you don't enjoy being with me, Jenna. It's there in your eyes.' His voice dropped to a husky murmur that did terrible things to her concentration.

'It's there in the way you turn into my caress whenever I touch you.' He palmed her cheek and her eyes flickered shut at the sheer pleasure of that skin-to-skin contact. 'It's there when you kiss me.'

Jenna felt his breath on her lips and snapped her eyes open, turning her head and sidestepping just as he bent to kiss her.

'This is nonsense, Jenna. I want you. I'm not ashamed of it. Is it so awful that I want to keep you here?'

Her mouth wobbled and she bit her bottom lip, horrified at the welling emotion that threatened to reduce her to a quivering wreck. She would *not* break down in front of him.

'Not awful for you,' she croaked out in a voice not her own. 'But it is for me. I'm ashamed of what I'd become if I agreed.' Jenna blinked gritty eyes and turned her head, meeting his stare straight on.

'*Scusi*?' He looked utterly uncomprehending. 'What are you talking about?'

Her mouth firmed. 'You know exactly what I'm talking about, Fabrizio. I've got too much pride to become your paid mistress. Once was enough. I don't ever want to go there again.'

'I never paid you. You wouldn't accept anything from me.' If anything he looked furious that she'd rejected his cash and expensive gifts of jewellery.

She shook her head. 'Except a roof over my head, meals, clothes, hospitality. I let you pay my way for the months we were together. I lived off you.'

He threw up his arms. 'We were lovers, Jenna. What did you expect? That I'd charge you rent for sharing my bed? Be reasonable.'

'I'm not the one being unreasonable, Fabrizio. You ask too much of me. You ask me to give up my self-respect.'

He stared at her as if he'd never seen her before. 'You say being my lover *degrades* you?' He drew himself up to his full, imposing height, making her more than ever aware of his potent strength. 'You insult me.'

Jenna wrapped her arms around her torso. She was breaking apart inside. The pain had gone from gnawing discomfort to ragged, tearing anguish.

'I'm sure there are plenty of women who'd be honoured to accept what you offer, Fabrizio, but it's not enough for me. I'm worth more.'

'You want to haggle over a financial settlement?' He scowled down at her and she laughed at how far off the mark he was.

'I mean I value myself more highly than you do. I won't be relegated to some hole in the corner affair, to be brushed aside and belittled.'

'I never—'

'You did, Fabrizio.' Jenna rubbed her hands up her bare arms, trying to create some warmth where there was only an icy chill. 'You took a phone call. An invitation to your mother's birthday celebration.' She paused, swallowing. 'Obviously the caller asked if you planned to bring me with you but you declined. You said, if I remember correctly,' and she did remember – the words were engraved in her brain, 'that you had no intention of taking your *mistress* to an intimate family celebration.'

His eyes widened.

'But I wasn't supposed to hear that, was I? I was supposed to be grateful the mighty scion of the Armati family deigned to share his bed with a nobody like me. Or perhaps I was supposed to be dazzled by the promise of riches to come?'

'That's why you left me?' He looked thunder-struck. 'It wasn't like that.'

'It was exactly like that, Fabrizio. I wasn't good enough to meet your mother because I was your mistress.' She paused and dragged in a breath. Some-how she couldn't seem to fill her lungs. 'What a quaint, old-fashioned word that is. Why not whore or slut? They mean the same, after all.'

Pain lashed her. Not from the sound of such ugly words on her tongue but the fact that was how he'd thought of her, with such disdain. He'd turned the heady joy she'd experienced into something tainted.

And, glutton for punishment, she'd let him drag her into his world again. Oh, she'd gone willingly because she hadn't had the willpower to resist him and she'd told herself this time *she* set the rules. But standing here in his aristocratic home, surrounded by wealth that had taken centuries to accumulate and looking into his stunned face, Jenna knew she'd made the biggest mistake of her life.

Nothing would ever fix this.

'Don't talk like that.' His soft, persuasive tone was replaced by sharp command. 'It doesn't suit you, Jenna. You're turning this into something it isn't.

You don't understand.'

Jenna backed away from him, knowing she couldn't take any more.

'Oh, I understand perfectly. There's nothing you can say that will change the truth. So don't bother trying.' She stared into his shocked, gorgeous face one last time, imprinting his features on her memory, then turned away. 'Goodbye, Fabrizio.'

Chapter Seven

'FABRIZIO, ARE YOU STILL WITH me?'
He blinked as a slim hand waved in front of his face and the tiny trattoria came back into focus. Suddenly he heard the clatter of lunchtime dishes and the distant hum of conversation. 'There's no need for theatrics, Chiara.'

His sister puffed out an exasperated breath, rolling her dark eyes and pushing her hair back behind her ears. 'You were miles away. You weren't paying attention at all.'

'Do you honestly expect me to hang on every word when you insist on describing your shopping trip in excruciating detail?' Catching her eye, he couldn't quite repress a half smile. 'A man has his limits, even a long-suffering brother.'

'But that's not why you're distracted, is it?' Chiara said with discomfiting insight. 'There's something wrong.'

He looked down at the menu, tension setting hard across his shoulders. 'Have you decided what you want to eat?'

'It's not like you to hide from a problem.'

'Who says I've got a problem?' he growled, but his heart wasn't in it. Jenna's words sat like a lump of cold lead in his belly. The pain in her beautiful eyes was branded onto his brain. Had he really been so selfish? He shifted uncomfortably in his seat.

'I do. I've never seen you like this. Is it the company? Has there been some disaster you haven't mentioned?'

Fabrizio gestured dismissively. 'Business is booming. It's outperforming all the trends.'

'Are you sick? Is that it?' She reached out across the table.

'Of course I'm not sick. I'm never ill. Now about this meal—'

'If you haven't been diagnosed with something horrible and business is thriving, what else could it be?' Chiara sat back, her eyes narrowing on his face, her head tilting to one side. Suddenly her eyes opened wide. 'I don't believe it,' she whispered. 'I really don't believe it. It's a woman, isn't it? After all these years some woman has finally got to you.' She shook her head. 'I never thought I'd see the day you felt something for one of them.'

Fabrizio's mouth flattened. 'You make me sound like some sort of Casanova.'

Her eyebrows arched. 'If the shoe fits, big brother. You've been loving and leaving them for as long as I can remember. Except I doubt *love* entered into it, for you at least.'

Fabrizio sat straighter, scowling. 'You think I've left a trail of broken hearts?' He shook his head. He'd always taken the precaution of choosing sophisticated women who understood he enjoyed sex, enjoyed female companionship, but had no intention of settling down yet.

Until Jenna.

With her he'd taken one look and known he had

to have her. There'd been no time for carefully setting the boundaries, just a gut-deep certainty he needed her.

He *still* needed her.

'Well,' Chiara paused, 'a string of disappointed women. I can think of at least two who were horribly let down when you ditched them.'

Fabrizio stared. 'You knew them?'

'They were hardly a secret.' Her look was assessing. 'Until lately. For ages I've heard reports about a beautiful blonde with a great smile but you've kept her very much to yourself.'

A great smile. Jenna's smile could light up a room. It always warmed him. It had been one of the things that had first drawn him to her. Now his world felt cold without her.

His heart dived. Last time he'd seen her those lush lips had been quivering in distress – so at odds with the bravado of her angled chin and perfect poise. Pain slashed through his belly, ripping a gaping hole that left him raw and bleeding. He was to blame for that.

'Fabrizio?' He looked up to see Chiara watching him closely, her brow puckered. 'Why didn't I meet her? Why did you kept her to yourself?'

Because she was different.

Because Jenna wasn't like the other women who flitted in and out of his life.

Because, instinctively he'd known she was more important than all the rest. Even if he hadn't wanted to acknowledge it.

Santo cielo! He ploughed his hand through his hair.

'Fabrizio!'

He felt Chiara's hand on his sleeve and met round, questioning eyes.

'Are you all right?' For once his little sister looked serious, all teasing gone.

He shook his head. 'Anything but.' He hauled in a rough breath that made his tight lungs ache. 'I've made the biggest mistake of my life.'

Chapter Eight

'*P*RONTO.' JENNA HELD THE PHONE to her ear with one hand while she rubbed the blackened brass door-knob with the other.

'Jenna, it's Adriana here from the Tourist Office.'

Jenna sat back on her heels and wiped her sleeve over her damp forehead. She'd worked steadily all morning and ached all over. This call was a welcome respite, even if she could barely afford the time.

'Adriana! How are you?'

'Good, thank you.' Her friend sounded breathless. 'But I have news. Your first guests are on their way.'

Jenna's eyes widened. 'Not for another week. By then I'll have finished—'

'You don't have another week. This was too good an opportunity to pass up, believe me. Just tell me you've got the internet connection up and running. That's a must for them, apparently.'

'Of course I have. I was working on the website again this last week. But I'm not ready for guests.'

'You'll have to be. They're on their way, said they'd be there in an hour.'

Jenna shot to her feet, leaving her stomach on the floor. An hour? Impossible. She looked at the ladder and bucket on the front step, thought of the unfinished painting in the dining room, all the work to be done before she could open her guesthouse.

'You'll have to call them back and tell them there's been a mistake.'

'And turn down the chance for triple the income you'd get from a full house?'

Jenna slumped against the wall. 'Say that again.'

'That's the whole point. I warned them you weren't planning to open till next week but they brushed that aside. There's only three of them but they want complete privacy. They're willing to book the whole guesthouse at three times the usual rate just to ensure they're alone.'

'Who are they? Royalty incognito or something?' Though what royalty would be doing in her little slice of rural Tuscany, Jenna had no idea.

'I don't think so. The guy I spoke to was a Frederico Santarelli. The name wasn't familiar to me.'

'Me neither.' Jenna glanced at her watch, calculating when Signor Santarelli might appear. 'Are you sure he was serious? About the money, I mean?'

She wasn't really considering opening her doors today, was she?

'Dead serious. All he seemed concerned with was a guarantee of complete privacy and internet access.'

'How long do they want to stay?'

'A month initially.'

'A month?' Jenna yelped, her mind whirling at the prospect of such an injection of cash into her stretched bank account. She'd estimated how long it would take to begin breaking even with her new business. But with unexpected guests paying the equivalent of three months' full income in one hit…

How could she say no?

'Thanks, Adriana. I'll call you back later.'

Jenna ended the call and sped into action, clearing the hallway, hiding mops and tools, then washing her hands before racing up the stairs to the guest bedrooms. Just as well she'd finished several of the bedrooms. At least her surprise guests would have somewhere comfortable and luxurious to sleep. She grabbed the pristine, lavender-dried sheets and began making the four-poster bed in the first room.

Fifty-five minutes later, Jenna was pinning up her hair, her body still slightly damp from her quick shower, when she heard the low growl of a motor. Rapidly she pulled on a tailored, dark skirt and an aquamarine shirt she knew matched her eyes, then slipped into her black heels and added her mother's pearl earrings. One thing she'd learnt, presentation was everything. If these wealthy guests were paying for the luxury of complete seclusion, they'd expect an elegant hostess, not a bedraggled navvy in paint-stained clothes.

One final glance in the mirror as she tucked in her shirt and she was out the door, heading towards the entrance hall.

She was on the bottom step when the front door swung open, letting in a blaze of light that silhouetted a dark figure. A tall, imposing figure that for a moment made her heart stall. Till she realised how foolish the very notion that Fabrizio Armati would follow her into the depths of the Tuscan countryside. Imagine him risking his precious Lamborghini on her rutted, not-yet-repaired drive!

'Signor Santarelli?' She stepped forward, a welcoming smile on her face.

'Not quite,' said the voice that haunted her dreams.

Jenna slammed to a stop, her hand pressing against her frantically pounding heart. Her indrawn breath was overloud in the silence.

'Fabrizio?' His name was a bare scratch of sound. She blinked into the light. 'What are you doing here?'

Silly how hope rose, like a flame out of sheer darkness. Pleasure soared through her, only to be shot down in cinders as memories crowded in. There could be no happy ending for them.

He stepped inside, closing the door behind him and Jenna saw the expensive case he carried. He crossed the hall to where she stood, transfixed, then deliberately planted his suitcase at the foot of the stairs.

'No!' This couldn't be happening. It couldn't be real. 'You can't—'

'I can. You're already expecting me.'

Her head swung from side to side in denial even as she ate him up. He looked utterly gorgeous, suave in his hand-made suit yet utterly masculine with that dangerous glint in his piercing grey eyes.

It took far too long for his words to register. She stiffened. 'No, I'm waiting for a Signor Santarelli.'

'My assistant. He made the booking.'

Jenna swayed a little as that sank in and she grabbed for the newel post, smooth and reassuringly strong beneath her unsteady fingers. 'That can't be. There are supposed to be three guests.'

'There will be, later. For now it's just me.'

His gaze never left hers and, unbidden, a sizzle of heat flared in her veins even though his expression was sombre, not seductive. In fact, he looked as grim as she'd ever seen him. Not angry or haughty, but as if he carried the weight of the world on those wide shoulders. He looked weary around the eyes too, like he'd been getting far less than the usual few hours' sleep he needed in order to function.

'You can't stay here.' Jenna didn't care how much money she'd lose by turning him away. She couldn't have Fabrizio under the same roof. It would be like rubbing salt into an open wound. This was her fresh start – a place with no memories of Fabrizio to haunt it. 'What were you thinking?'

'That I wanted to see you.' He lifted his hand as if to touch her face and she shrank back. Instantly he stiffened and she almost convinced herself that was pain she saw flicker across his face.

'You can't just walk in here and expect to take up where we left off.' Her tone was bitter, her throat raw with pain.

'I never expected anything so simple.' He paused and she had the oddest sensation he hesitated, searching for the right words. That couldn't be right. Fabrizio was assured and persuasive, never lost for words.

'You'd better go.' She made to step past him, her eyes on the front door, when he stopped her.

He didn't use force, just reached out and grazed her wrist with the back of his hand. Instantly her senses went into overdrive and she stumbled to a dead stop. Her chest rose and fell quickly, mirroring her agitation. She had to fight to keep her eyelids from fluttering shut at the delicious torment of that light-as-air caress.

Despair filled her. Even now she had no defences against him. She'd tried and tried but nothing, not time nor distance nor anger had worked.

'Please, Jenna. We have to talk.'

Her head jerked around, dragged by the pleading note she'd never heard from Fabrizio.

This close, his eyes glowed with a heat that threatened to incinerate her. She tried to pull away but stood, rooted to the spot. Finally, swallowing hard, she nodded.

'In here.'

Reluctantly she led the way to the room off the hallway. Her legs felt stiff, like she'd forgotten how to put one foot in front of the other.

'I approve,' he murmured behind her and she spun around to see him surveying the watered lemon silk on three walls, the full-length bookcases taking up the other one, and comfortable lounges grouped before the fireplace and near the window. 'You've made this very inviting.'

Any other time she'd have been thrilled by his praise. When she'd bought the villa with the money she'd inherited from her parents and her hefty new mortgage, this room had been dark and neglected. It had taken lots of hard work and careful planning to turn it into a luxury retreat on her modest budget.

At least she'd had more success with her makeover than she had at eradicating Fabrizio from her thoughts.

'You didn't come here to discuss my taste in furnishings.' She planted her hands on her hips, trying to hide the way her blood ricocheted too fast around her body just at the sight of him.

'How *did* you come to be here? You were supposed to be working for De Laurentis.'

Her eyebrows rose. Fabrizio sounded almost accusing, as if she'd cheated him somehow.

'I told you, I didn't want to work in a large, city hotel.' Not that he'd remember that. He'd been too caught up in his own demands to consider what she wanted. He hadn't listened to her at all when he'd thrown out his offer, no, his demand, that she work for him in Rome. 'My dream has always been to work somewhere small enough to provide a special, memorable experience for guests.'

She didn't confide that the true catalyst for her resignation was a broken heart. Exciting as the job was that Luca De Laurentis had offered, Jenna had known she had to escape, find somewhere far away from the cosmopolitan cities frequented by Fabrizio. This ramshackle old villa set in the Tuscan hills had been a godsend, even if it had used up every cent she possessed and put her in a lifetime of debt.

She had her dream, she reminded herself fiercely. That was all that mattered.

'That explains how long it took to find you.'

'Find me?' she parroted, frowning.

Of course he looked for you. It's no coincidence he's here.

Yet the idea of Fabrizio searching her out again seemed ridiculously improbable. He'd watched her walk out his door and hadn't lifted a finger to stop her. He hadn't uttered a word.

'Why are you here, Fabrizio?' She stood tall, one hand planted on the back of a massive wing chair. She told herself he couldn't know she needed the support for her wobbly legs.

For long seconds he held her gaze from across the room. He shoved his hands deep in his trouser pockets, looking far too sexy and appealing for her peace of mind.

'I came to tell you I was wrong.'

Wrong?

Fabrizio was the ultimate macho Italian male, confident and certain of his own infallibility. She didn't think such a word was in his vocabulary.

While she was trying to absorb that, he closed the space between them and suddenly his hands were there, threading his fingers through hers. She shivered as her body locked down, shocked by the depth of her response.

'I was wrong not to take you with me to that family celebration.'

Jenna bit her lip. 'It wasn't just about missing out on the party.'

'I know. It was because I dismissed you.' He breathed deep. 'I hurt you, deeply, and for that I apologise, *tesoro*. You deserved better from me.'

Jenna's eyes widened as she took in his intent expression. 'You're right. I did.' For a moment she hovered on the brink of hope, then made herself face reality. Overdue as it was, it wasn't his apology she needed. 'But I've moved on.' She tried to withdraw her hands but his hold was unbreakable.

She frowned. 'Fabrizio?'

'It was a first for me, you see, and I didn't deal with it well.' He laughed, the short jab of sound harsh and unsettling in the breathless room. 'Didn't deal with it well, now that's an understatement! It threw me for a loop. It was all so completely new.'

'Fabrizio? What are you talking about?' Jenna had never seen him look or sound like this.

His eyes gleamed in a way that snatched her breath.

'The way you make me feel, *tesoro*. The way you've made me feel from the first, even in Venice when I missed my meeting. I saw you sitting alone at that café and I couldn't walk past. I had to spend the day with you.'

And the night. And every night after while the magic had lasted.

But Jenna knew it had been an illusion. He'd reduced what they shared to just sex.

'I won't be your mistress again, Fabrizio.' Her low voice was unsteady. She couldn't take much more.

'It's not a mistress I want.'

'Then what do you want? Forgiveness?' Finally Jenna managed to jerk her hands free and backed away, putting space between them. 'I accept your apology. All right? Now I want you to leave.'

'I can't.' His voice was low and urgent. 'I tried keeping my distance and it was the biggest mistake of my life.' He stopped and hauled in a breath that lifted his whole chest. 'I love you, Jenna, and I can't hide from it anymore.'

'Love?' Her eyes stretched wide. Her heart thundered in her chest. 'You don't love me, Fabrizio. You don't know the meaning of the word.'

Sharply he nodded. '*Sì*. That was the problem.' A wide hand gesture emphasised his words. 'I was used to sex and simple, undemanding companionship. I wasn't used to *feelings*.' He frowned, his gaze piercing. 'I didn't want to admit what you made me feel, or that you meant more to me than any woman ever had.'

'You had a fine way of showing it.' Jenna told herself she wouldn't fall for his easy words, no matter how tempting.

He nodded and ploughed his hand back through his glossy dark hair, leaving it in gorgeous disarray. 'I'm ashamed of that, Jenna. When my sister asked if I was bringing you to the party, there was suddenly no escaping what you meant to me. How important you were to my happiness. It hit me out of the blue and it scared the hell out of me.'

He spun on his foot and paced across the room and back. 'I hadn't let myself think about it before, and when I did my first reaction was to deny it.'

Jenna swallowed hard, trying to take in his explanation. Was it possible?

The idea of Fabrizio floundering and scared didn't seem real.

'You called me your mistress because you were scared of me?' She folded her arms. 'That doesn't seem likely.'

He shrugged, his hands spreading. 'It was a knee-jerk reaction. I wasn't ready to settle down with one woman for the rest of my life.'

Jenna stared. 'Settle down?' Had she missed something? 'You never mentioned that.' She felt dazed, as if she'd walked into a foreign place where dreams, even outrageously improbable ones, could come true.

His lips quirked up in a smile that did outrageous things to her insides. 'I hadn't got to that yet. But since you mention it, I want to share my life with you, Jenna. Permanently.'

He stepped close and lifted his hand to feather a caress across her cheek. The tenderness of that gesture threatened to make her knees collapse.

'Fabrizio!' She couldn't prevent the needy whisper and his smile widened.

'Be mine, Jenna. Marry me.'

'Marry you?' Stunned, she stared up into an expression suddenly turned serious.

'*Sì*. All these months apart have only proved what I was too cowardly to admit before, that I love you. I can't live without you. I want you as my wife.' His hand slid down her arm and meshed with hers. His grip was firm but somehow sustaining.

It took a long time to find her voice. Even the touch of his hand didn't feel quite real as she stared up at him. 'You want me to marry you when you can't even introduce me to your family?' That still stung.

As did the glimmer of humour in his eyes. 'Ah, about that. You'll meet them soon enough. My assistant booked accommodation for three people. My mother and sister will be here next week, after we've had time to sort ourselves out.'

'They're coming here?' It was one shock piled on another. She shook her head, trying to absorb it all.

'They want to meet you. They want to help plan the wedding.'

Jenna drew herself up, frowning. Her emotions were all over the place, indignation vying for prominence with hope, fear and disbelief. 'You were so sure I'd say yes that you told them we were marrying?'

'No, my love.' His hand squeezed hers and her heart tumbled over, making a mockery of her doubts. How wonderful that sounded. *My love.* 'I told them how I felt and that I wasn't sure if you'd have me. My mother, being my mother, was sure I'd convince you, and decided it was time to meet her future daughter-in-law. But my sister said she was coming so she could watch me squirm. She said she hoped you'd make me work for what I wanted.'

'I like the sound of your sister.' Right now she needed an ally. Fabrizio was turning her world on its head and she was scared to believe all this was real.

He nodded, a hint of a smile in the grooves bracketing his mouth. 'I'm afraid you two are going to get on far too well.'

Slowly he drew her to him, and Jenna found herself in the circle of his arms. Suddenly her indignation bled away. In truth this was exactly where she wanted to be.

'I love you, Jenna. I want to be with you for the rest of my life.'

'I…' Even now, with her heart almost bursting with joy, she hesitated. 'It's all a bit overwhelming and sudden.'

Fabrizio nodded, but he didn't smile. 'We have all the time we want. The rest of my things will arrive next week.'

'More suitcases?'

'And office equipment.' He took a deep breath. 'I plan to work from here. I'm assured you've got internet access. And I'd pay to rent the space. And for accommodation for my assistant. But he won't arrive for a month. I'm taking a break from business till then.'

Jenna gawped. Fabrizio take a break from business? It was unheard of.

'You want to work from here? Run your business from a guesthouse? But I'll be working. I'll be busy with guests.'

'Which will give me time to see to my own business.' He paused, his voice deepening. 'And we'll have the nights together.' That bass note vibrated across her flesh, making it tingle in sensual awareness.

'But we're deep in the country. Nowhere near Rome!'

Fabrizio shrugged, his mouth pulled up at one side in the sexiest half smile she'd ever seen. 'What does one wear in the country? You'll have to teach me, *tesoro*. I suspect not my usual suits. And I will have to insist on repairing that sorry excuse for a driveway. My poor car.' He shook his head mournfully.

'You're serious!' Jenna breathed in shock. 'You really want to live here with me?'

He nodded, hauling her close, till her body melded with his hard frame and her head rested on his shoulder. 'I can't let you go. Even if it takes the rest of my life for you to return my feelings. I want to be with you.' The words rumbled up from deep within him so she felt them as well as heard them.

'You don't have to wait, Fabrizio.' She arched back, meeting his eyes. Suddenly she was happier than she'd ever thought possible. It felt like the sunshine outdoors had somehow found a way to stream straight into her heart. 'I've loved you from the moment I looked up to see you at my table in Venice. I've never stopped loving you.'

'*Amore mio*! You love me? You loved me since then?' His eyes blazed, his arms tightening around her.

Yet his expression held a hint of doubt. 'Are you certain? After the way I treated you?'

'I've never been more certain of anything in my life.' Standing here, in Fabrizio's arms, was the only place she wanted to be.

'I don't deserve you.' His voice held an unfamiliar hollow note. Never had she heard Fabrizio so self-effacing. The man she knew was always sure of himself.

Jenna put her hand to his chest and felt the thunder of his heartbeat beneath her palm. It matched the beat of her own. 'I love you, Fabrizio. Forever. There was never any doubt. The amazing thing is that you never realised.'

Slowly a smile curled across his lips, driving deep grooves down his cheeks and stealing her breath, leaving her dazzled.

'You make me the happiest man in Italy. In the world.' He pulled her even closer and her knees turned to water with happiness and excitement. 'You'll marry me?'

'I hadn't thought as far ahead as marriage, but—'

'But you will let me persuade you, *sì*?' His grin was pure triumphant, sexy male and she melted a little in his hold.

'I'll look forward to that,' she murmured, knowing already that it was precisely what she wanted.

'So will I, *carissima*.' Then his head dipped till their lips met and Jenna gave up thinking. There was plenty of time for that later. A lifetime of it, together.

BOUGHT BY

The Italian

Book 2, Hot Italian Nights

*For all those readers who read
Fabrizio's story and wanted his sister, Chiara's.
Thank you for your support.*

*And for Josephine Chiara Caporetto –
I promised you Chiara as a heroine one day!
Hope you enjoy this one.*

Chapter One

GENNARO DE LAURENTIS PLANTED HIM-SELF at the rear of the huge reception room, eyes fixed on the spotlit dais.

Around him the crowd chattered in rising excitement. The charity auction had morphed abruptly from mildly interesting, just another date on the Milan social calendar, to enthralling.

All because of Chiara Armati.

The prospect of buying the vivacious beauty, if just for a dinner date, roused even the most unimaginative.

Bidding had started in the thousands of euros.

Then Chiara herself had gone to the podium, sashaying through the packed room. The spotlight tracked her progress and the play of flame-red fabric over the flare of her hips and tight buttocks. Every man in the room watched the cling and shift of that sexy dress and her even sexier body, as she squeezed past the tables and up to the stage.

Gennaro's chest constricted. His hands clenched, his jaw locking.

He hated other men slavering over her.

He hated that she'd agreed to be auctioned off. Even if strict stipulations clarified it was only a few hours of her time, her charming company, being sold. The winner would have her to himself over dinner in Milan's best restaurant.

Heat spiked in Gennaro's belly as he watched the crowd watch her.

The testosterone levels in the room rose and peaked as she stood, smiling, beside the compere.

Her glossy, sable hair was pulled back from that exquisitely sensual face, emphasising her bone-deep beauty. Bare arms and shoulders glowed under the brilliant lighting that accentuated every lush curve in her slender body.

He ground his teeth as she laughed up at something the host said, her face alight. It was her laughter that had first attracted Gennaro.

He wanted to cover her. Wrap his jacket around her shoulders and cart her off the stage. By force if necessary.

She was his.

Correction. She'd been his.

Until the day she'd stormed out of his home, her fine patrician nose so far in the air it was a wonder she hadn't tripped herself up.

He shouldn't have let her go. He'd known she was volatile, but he hadn't credited she'd walk out and never return.

As if she could pretend what they'd shared was over!

A collective gasp filled the room and he forced himself to focus on the bidding.

'Forty thousand euros.' A media mogul with a satisfied smirk nodded, acknowledging the crowd's applause.

'Fifty thousand.' A tall man to one side offered.

Chiara's head swung around to him. Was that relief on her face? If so it was quickly masked.

'Sixty.' The mogul bid again, frowning. Clearly he expected to get what he wanted. By all accounts he always got what he wanted, even if it bordered on the illegal or immoral.

Gennaro's mouth tightened. He didn't like the way the man leered up at her.

'Seventy.'

'Eighty.'

The murmurs of the audience subsided as the bidding rose. The sums offered were unexpected, even for the company of a gorgeous woman, an up and coming fashion designer and a member of one of Rome's oldest families.

Gennaro rocked back on his heels as the tall man at the side of the room bid again, so high there was a gasp of astonishment then a buzz of excited anticipation.

Gennaro smiled grimly as Chiara, for once visibly disconcerted, grabbed the auctioneer's lectern as if for support.

Who'd have thought it? For the first time ever her self-assurance looked shaky. Long ago her ancestors had bargained for their personal slaves in the market. She would be the first Armati to be bought that way. Had that finally dented her gilt-edged sense of superiority?

The bidding closed to a round of thunderous applause and a standing ovation. No one in the history of the charity event had ever bid so much on a single lot. Across the room Chiara smiled and applauded. The victorious bidder gave a quick, almost nervous bow from the side of the room.

But Gennaro's attention was all for Chiara. He guessed no one else in the vast room could tell how shaken she was. Society darling and privileged aristocrat, Chiara Armati was used to being adored. But the swift escalation of the bidding from high to astronomical had thrown her. Even from this distance he sensed her nerves, her wariness.

Gennaro had become an expert at reading her moods. He knew her as no-one outside her family did, more intimately than any other man.

But Chiara still had much to learn about him.

Fire branded his belly, building to a white hot burn. She'd stamped those dainty feet all over him as she stalked out the door. Had she truly believed he'd take that lying down?

He smiled, anticipation welling as he turned and left the room.

Chiara sipped sparkling water, trying to find her equilibrium as her companions' animated chatter washed over her. She'd returned to their table the focus of rampant speculation.

What had begun as a favour to a friend, agreeing to dine with a stranger for a charity donation, had become a profoundly unsettling experience.

Raised in the public eye due to her family's lineage and wealth, she'd thought herself inured to such attention. She'd even thought the auction might raise the profile of her fledgling design business.

But being bid over in public, and so aggressively, like a harem girl bought for a pasha's pleasure, had unnerved her. It wasn't being looked at by so many people that bothered her. She was used to that. It was the *way* they'd watched her, with an avid excitement that had turned a charitable gesture into something sleazy. As if, when the bids rose to incredible heights, everyone believed far more than an innocent meal was on offer.

As if *she'd* been for sale.

Chiara wished she'd brought a wrap for her halter neck evening dress. She'd wanted to cover up, especially when Enrico Contaldo in the front row had leered up at her, smacking his lips as if she were some tasty morsel.

She shivered and swallowed another mouthful of water.

But that hadn't been the worst. Far worse had been the instant when she'd caught sight of a dark silhouette at the back of the room. A tall man with powerful shoulders who stood unmoving through the whole spectacle. Dazzled by the light, she'd still been almost sure it was him, the man she'd once believed in. The man she'd foolishly given her heart to.

That heart had instantly leapt in excitement and hope, recognising that against the odds, he was here for *her*.

But the latecomer had given no indication he was interested in bidding for the privilege of her company.

Sick to the pit of her stomach, Chiara told herself it couldn't have been Gennaro. If it had been, the fact he'd let the slimy media baron bid for her spoke volumes. Gennaro had used her for his own ends. He had no interest in her personally. She'd been a convenient stepping stone to getting what he wanted – insider information.

Familiar pain pierced. It had been weeks since

she'd discovered the truth. Yet she still felt as raw and desperate as the day she'd pleaded with him to tell her it was all a mistake, that he'd never betray her.

What an idiot she'd been.

Chiara cringed and reached, not for her water, but her tall flute of champagne. Recklessly she knocked back a huge gulp. Surely that would help deaden the hurt. There was still a long way to go before this evening was over.

'Signorina Armati?' She turned to find one of the event's organisers at her side.

'Yes?' She took another sip of bubbly.

'I have a favour to ask.'

He looked uncertain and she nodded encouragingly. 'Yes?'

'It's rather unusual but not against the conditions of the prize.'

The prize. That was her. Remarkable how viscerally she reacted to the sensation of being bought like a chattel.

'Yes?' She wished he'd get to the point and leave her to nurse her bruised emotions.

'Signor Fabbri, the bidder who won the pleasure of your company for dinner, has a request.'

Chiara stilled. What had he asked that made the event organiser look so tentative? 'Go on.'

'He asked if you would consider missing the auction dinner here.' He nodded to the door on the far side of the room where waiters were emerging with the first course. 'He would like to invite you to dine with him tonight instead. The original agreement was to meet at the end of the week, but he thought, since you were both here…'

Chiara hesitated. Go out with him tonight? All she wanted was to head back to her hotel and find some peace and solitude.

On the other hand, dining with this Signor Fabbri now meant she didn't have to come back to Milan later. More importantly, her obligation to him would be over. The sooner the better, as far as she was concerned.

Plus it would give her a reason to escape the stares of the fascinated crowd that she still felt trained on her. If she stayed here it would be a long, drawn out evening, with the auction continuing between courses.

Relief filled her at the excuse to leave. A few hours now and she could put all this behind her.

'Of course.' She pinned on her most gracious smile. 'Tell Signor Fabbri I'd be happy to.'

Ten minutes later Chiara found herself being ushered to the car by the tall stranger with the long face and surprisingly gentle eyes who'd stunned Milan society with his extravagant bidding.

Older than her by several years, his manner instantly put her at ease. She'd expected someone brasher and more self-satisfied, since he'd faced down the media giant, Contaldo, without even blinking. But this man was polite to the point of self-effacement. His old-fashioned manners, opening doors and all but bowing her from the room, soothed her ruffled feathers. Chiara relaxed a fraction.

Together they descended the wide stairs to the street.

'Ah, here's the car now.' He gestured to a dark sports car pulling up at the pavement.

Chiara stared, surprised. Signor Fabbri, though obviously wealthy, hadn't struck her as the type to drive a sports car. This was the sort of powerful, designer car her brother Fabrizio would drive, or—

No. She'd promised herself she wasn't going to think about Gennaro again.

'Do we need to drive? It's only a few blocks to the restaurant.' Chiara breathed deep, glad to be out of the closed atmosphere of the reception room. The noise and mingled scents of expensive perfumes, or perhaps the unexpected stress of the auction, made her grateful for the balmy summer air. Far better to be outside, enjoying the soft early evening light.

'As you say, it's not far. But with those shoes…' He shrugged, his eyes flickering down to her high, spiked red heels with their slender ankle straps and faux flowers that perfectly matched her evening gown.

He really was considerate. Perhaps an evening spent in his company wouldn't be such a chore.

He opened the car door and she smiled, delighted and relieved that this evening promised to be so easy after all, when she'd been dreading it. 'That's very thoughtful of you. Thank you.'

'Allow me.' He stood between her and the car, gesturing for her to pass over her purse. 'I'll stow this for you. You may need to balance yourself as the seat is so low.' Again that slight flicker of his gaze downward.

Chiara liked his attentiveness and the fact he didn't stare. This dress, a new design, looked great but wasn't made for climbing in and out of low slung supercars.

'Thank you.' She passed over her purse and watched him lean in, passing it to the shadowy valet driver. Then Signor Fabbri turned and steadied her as she sank down into the embrace of the soft leather seat. Carefully she swivelled, surprised at the amount of leg room in the vehicle, as he gently shut the passenger door for her.

Instantly the engine revved. Through the throaty growl Chiara heard another sound, the small click of the door locks. She frowned, looking up through the side window at Signor Fabbri. Instead of walking around to the driver's side he stood on the pavement, his long face grave.

Unease trickled down her backbone as the engine growled again.

'You'd better put on your seatbelt, princess,' said a familiar voice. No-one else had a voice quite like it: whisky and honey, husky yet smooth. Machismo and pure seduction.

The trickle became a full-scale floodtide of shock as she swung her head around and saw a familiar profile.

Gennaro De Laurentis. The man who'd used and betrayed her.

The man she'd never wanted to see again.

Chapter Two

'**P**ULL OVER. NOW.' HER VOICE rose on the final word and she snapped her mouth closed, rather than betray how he'd stunned her.

In answer Gennaro accelerated through some traffic lights, one hand, she saw now, stashing her silk purse further down between his seat and the driver's side door.

'And give me back my purse.'

Even in profile she saw his eyebrow hike up. 'What happened to "please", princess? Or aren't you familiar with the word?'

'I wouldn't waste my breath. Not on someone like *you,*' she spat with all the venom in her wounded soul.

To her chagrin the man beside her didn't react. But then why should he? She could only dent his ego if he actually cared about her. And everything they'd shared had been false, at least on his part.

It flayed her that she'd been so taken in by him. She who'd been awake since her teens to the devious, grasping ways of men interested in her social standing or money or connections, or even just a quick lay.

'Well, now that we've established your sense of superiority over a mere plebeian, perhaps you'd be so kind as to strap your seatbelt on.' His silky tone was infuriating.

'That's not necessary.' She lifted her chin. 'I have no intention of going anywhere with you, Signor De Laurentis.'

'Much as I hate to disappoint you, Chiara, you're not getting rid of me that easily.'

He flashed her a sideways look and she felt herself slump into the deep embrace of the bucket seat. Was it the way he said her name, in that velvet-on-gravel tone that reminded her of his bed, rumpled and smelling of sex? Or was it the impact of that indigo gaze? She'd always found his eyes captivating, their colour courtesy of his North Italian ancestors. This time his look sizzled. She felt it like fire, brushing her flesh.

She opened her mouth to argue then shut it again. There was no point. Gennaro had the keys, he'd locked the doors, and short of performing some desperate mime for a passing policeman, *if* she happened to see one, she had no choice but to stay where she was. Even her phone was out of reach thanks to Signor Fabbri.

'Who was he, the man at the auction?' She reached for the seatbelt and clicked it shut. 'A friend of yours?'

It took far too much effort to get the words out in a passably normal voice, rather than screech for him to stop right now. One look at that implacable jaw told her he wouldn't respond to persuasion or ultimatums.

'An employee.'

Chiara snorted. 'And there was I thinking he seemed quite pleasant! I should have guessed something wasn't right. His suit was good but not made for him. And anyone spending that sort of money…' Despite herself her gaze flicked to Gennaro, effortlessly suave in a dark jacket and open shirt that accentuated his aura of utterly masculine energy. Her stomach gave a dismaying lurch.

She was used to seeing him in faded jeans or motorcycle leathers. There'd been something about his rough-hewn earthiness, melded with his beautifully-sculpted features, that always made her throat catch. Now though, he looked a different man in his elegant clothes and sporting a close-cropped beard just long enough to be classed as more than stubble. It was shaped to reveal his sensuous mouth and accentuated the hard line of his jaw.

'Trust a spoiled blue-blood to judge people by their clothes.'

Chiara's hands curled into fists. The only people who carped on her lineage were those who envied it. Gennaro had never been one of them.

But he'd duped her once. She'd fallen for him but he hadn't cared. All he cared about was using her, taking the sensitive information she'd let slip about her brother's business and feeding it to *his* brother to beat him to a massively lucrative project. She'd never really known Gennaro. Who knew what he thought of her?

Pain clutched at her chest. She told herself she shouldn't care but the ache remained, spurring her anger.

'No, trust a fashion designer to tell how much clothes cost.' She sucked in a slow breath. 'Speaking of money, I hope the charity *is* going to get its payment out of this?'

'You're afraid I don't have the cash to cover your exorbitant purchase price?'

A ripple of atavistic fear coursed through her at the sheer smugness in his tone. As if he really *had* bought her, to do with as he pleased.

'I know you've got the cash.' But unlike most of the other people she knew, Gennaro De Laurentis didn't usually splash it about just for the sake of showing off his wealth. Going out with him she'd been as likely to find herself in a tiny back street café that served divine coffee and sweets, or on some deserted beach, where they could concentrate solely on each other, as at some ultra-trendy club.

She'd loved that. The unpredictability. The new experiences they'd shared. The sense their time together was about *them*, not about being seen.

Except it hadn't been about that at all, had it? Anguish filled her.

Mentally Chiara shook herself. How could she think back fondly to those times when all the while he'd been cleverly using her? She stiffened in her seat. 'I might not be sharing a meal with Signor Fabbri but you can't duck out of paying.'

'Oh, they'll get their payment, *cara*.' His low-voiced endearment was a lethal caress. Her breasts tightened and she cursed the fact her body still responded though her mind knew him for a cold-blooded fraud. 'I've bought you and I intend to get my money's worth. The deal still stands.'

No mistaking the darkly proprietorial satisfaction of his tone.

Chiara shuddered. It was too much, even for a woman pretending not to be fazed. The worst of it was her anger masked trepidation at this sudden, shocking turn of events.

'You haven't bought *me*.' Chiara paused, forcing the thread of dismay from her voice. She refused to let him see any hint of nerves despite the flock of sparrows wheeling and fluttering inside. 'The auction was merely for my company over dinner.'

'And I'm looking forward to that immensely.'

His complacent tone irked her.

'Well, in that case, Signor De Laurentis, I suggest you turn the car around. You're driving in the wrong direction for the restaurant.'

Not that she intended sitting across from him at a dining table. Once out of this car she'd be on her way, as far from him as she could get. How dare he dupe her like this? No doubt he was laughing over her gullibility just as he'd laughed at her innocence in falling for his lies.

To her horror, heat pricked her eyes. She swung her face towards the side window, the city streets a blur. Her mouth twisted. She wouldn't let him best her. She wouldn't!

'We're not dining there.' His voice was soft, as if he'd sensed her turmoil. She swallowed hard, hating the taste of disappointment clogging her mouth.

'Then where?' His response did nothing to allay her alarm.

'Somewhere private.'

Chiara closed her eyes. She was tired, she was upset. She didn't have the stamina to face this, face *him* tonight. She didn't want to be alone with Gennaro De Laurentis. Especially since the last few minutes had showed she wasn't yet immune to him.

'Chiara?' Ridiculous to think she heard concern in that deep voice.

'I don't want to be private with you.' From deep within she dredged the hatred that had bloomed out of shock and distress when he'd hurt her so badly. 'The rules of the auction specified a public place—'

'Stuff the rules.' He put his foot down, surging through another set of lights and heading for the autostrada.

'You're going out of town.' By a miracle Chiara kept her voice even as the buildings whipped by. She wasn't scared Gennaro would hurt her physically, never that. But it struck her suddenly that no-one except his co-conspirator had a clue where she was. The realisation was disturbing. Always she managed her own life. Even when they'd been lovers their meetings had been mutually agreed, fitting in with both their busy schedules.

'Yes.'

She gripped the soft leather of her seat with tense fingers, realising she didn't know this route. Had she ever felt so powerless?

'Where out of town?' Her voice took on the cool tone she'd learned in her youth when bothered by the press. It was perfect for masking insecurities.

'Somewhere we can talk.'

'Talk?' What had they to talk about? Surely it had all been said in Rome.

'Unless there's something else you'd rather do with me in private, princess?' His voice was pitched deep enough to reverberate through her belly, making her recall how impressively, how tenderly, he'd made love to her.

How she'd been taken in by him.

'There is, as a matter of fact.'

She sensed him dart a sideways stare her way. The powerful car shuddered for just a second as his grip changed on the steering wheel.

'And what's that?' She caught the tension in his voice, as if he actually cared. Instantly Chiara dismissed the notion. It was an illusion.

'I'd like–' she turned to look at him, reminding herself how he'd abused her trust '–to make you hurt. Badly.'

His bark of laughter surprised her. 'That's one thing I'll say for you, princess. You're not predictable.'

'Stop calling me that,' she ground out.

He shrugged and she dragged her gaze back to the view rather than watch the fluid movement of those broad shoulders. She'd always loved the latent strength of his powerful body, honed to perfection by years of hard labour on building sites. Even now he ran his own construction company, Gennaro was hands-on when he had the chance.

Hands-on.

Gennaro gave the phrase a whole new meaning. Chiara forced down the memory of his callused touch, so surprisingly gentle, tracking over her bare skin, drawing responses so intense they almost scared her.

Determinedly she stared at the view. They'd left the city behind. The car picked up speed.

'We're heading east.' Where were they going?

'*Brava*, princess.'

'I said I don't like that being called that.' It reminded her too much of the fawning hangers-on she and Fabrizio seemed to attract because of their family name. For years she'd searched for friends who cared about her, not her pedigree. She thought she'd found that in Gennaro. She shook her head. Well, it wasn't her pedigree he'd been interested in, she thought bitterly, just her link to her brother.

'My apologies, *cara*.'

She folded her arms across her chest, hating the way his endearment melted a little of the frost deep inside. It was that frost that helped her keep her chin up in this horrible, unbelievable situation.

'You realise that you have no right to take me anywhere?'

Silence.

'You may think you've bought my time because of the ridiculous amount of money you put down—'

'Ridiculous perhaps, but necessary. You're a hard woman to get near.'

It was Chiara's turn to shrug. 'My *friends* don't have any trouble.' Ice dripped from each syllable. She'd cut Gennaro from her life when she discovered what he'd done. That his "caring" was solely so he could get information about her brother's next commercial venture. No true friend, much less a lover, would behave as he had.

She paused, but he said nothing. Why should he? Whatever he wanted, it wasn't her friendship or approval. He'd destroyed any chance of regaining those well before today.

Chiara refused to let herself wonder what it was he wanted from her. Whatever it was, it couldn't be good if he had to resort to kidnap. Goosebumps broke out on her arms and she smoothed her hands over them, trying to get warm.

Instantly he leaned forward to adjust the air.

'I'm not going to hurt you, you know.' His voice was grave, just as if he'd read the fear churning inside her.

But there was more than one way of inflicting pain. It wasn't her physical self Chiara feared for. It was her heart. Already Gennaro De Laurentis had left a gaping hole in it.

'I want you to stop the car at the next service centre and let me out.'

Silence.

Was any man more infuriating? 'I agreed to dinner in a public restaurant. This.' She waved a hand at the luxury car speeding through the gathering gloom. 'This wasn't in the agreement.'

'So sue me.' Gennaro's silky tone stoked her anger.

'You think I won't?' She snapped out the words. 'You think I'll just sit back and let you drive me off into the night who knows where?' Her voice rose. 'This is abduction. It's a criminal offence.'

'Only if you complain about it to the police.'

'You can't seriously believe I won't.'

Again that shrug. 'Maybe I can persuade you not to.'

Chiara was so incensed she felt she'd explode. 'You think you're so persuasive I'll forget about you hijacking me? You've got to be kidding!' The man had an ego the size of Lake Como.

'I think despite your bluster you still have a soft spot for me.' He sounded appallingly sure of himself. 'I always could persuade you.'

The awful thing was he spoke the truth. He *had* been able to persuade her — into his bed, into enjoying herself with him when she should have devoted herself to the serious business of establishing her career.

Into trusting him with information she shouldn't have shared.

Chiara spluttered in frustration at his arrogance. She wanted to slap him. But he was driving at speed.

She wanted to shout and threaten but she knew it wouldn't dent his ego.

She wanted to throw something.

She sent him a coruscating glare. 'That was before I knew who and what you are.'

Deliberately she turned her shoulder and stared out the window.

Chapter Three

'WE'RE GOING EAST THEN NORTH.' The words were soft but Chiara could have sworn they were spoken through gritted teeth.

Good. He deserved to suffer too.

She parted her lips to ask where exactly he was taking her then thought better of it. She'd find out soon enough and the less she conversed with Gennaro De Laurentis, the better for her sanity.

She was furious with him. Shocked and anxious.

Yet at the same time a small unregenerate part of her felt… excited to be with him again. There was a sizzle in her blood she hadn't felt since she'd left him, an effervescence that didn't bode well for her self-control.

'You're not going to ask where in the north?' He paused. 'You're going to play childish games and not talk?'

Chiara's lips twitched but she stopped herself just in time from blurting out that he was the one playing games.

Silence for several more kilometres.

Despite the turmoil of her emotions, she sank back further into the moulded seat. The last hint of fear was dissolving now. This was too much like the evenings she'd spent with Gennaro when he'd driven them out of Rome at the end of the week for a passionate lovers' retreat.

Hurt dragged at her belly. She'd been so incandescently happy. She'd thought nothing could destroy that.

'We're going to the Alto Adige.'

Chiara's head swung round. 'That's ridiculous. It's hours away.' It was Italy's northernmost region, right up on the border with Austria and Switzerland. It was also one of the most remote places she knew, with the stark, beautiful Dolomite Mountains making travel slow between tiny mountain villages and ski resorts.

'You can spare me the time – for old times' sake.'

'I don't owe you anything.'

'Except dinner. I paid for the privilege, remember?' His voice was a honed blade.

'You're taking me to the Alps for dinner?'

'Why not? At least we'll be alone to talk.'

Chiara shivered. She didn't want to be alone with Gennaro. This close she breathed in his spicy, unique scent, like tangerines and cloves and hot, hard male.

She was afraid of that part of her that still craved him. How long before she was completely free of him?

'Why there?' But she could guess the answer. It was where he'd grown up. When he was a toddler his father died and his mother took him and his brothers back to her family in the north. To a tiny, distant village where some curious ancient mountain language was still the mother tongue and Italian was learnt in school. It had all sounded exotic and charming.

Now it sounded isolated.

'I've been working there, building a ski resort. It's a beautiful place and—'

'Let me guess, you thought I'd enjoy the view? At night?' Chiara's voice was ice-cold.

She glanced at the car's illuminated clock, telling herself whatever he was up to, she'd cope. Hadn't she coped with the shattering of her illusions, the crumbling of her dreams? The recollection put steel in her voice. 'We'll arrive in time for a midnight snack, not dinner, so I sincerely hope the meal is worth waiting for. You can wake me when we get there. By that time I'll be ready to eat. Despite the company.'

She shifted, turning away ostentatiously and letting her head flop against the head rest.

It was only in part an act. Stress and exhaustion were taking their toll. Every muscle ached with tension and her head throbbed.

Chiara shut her eyes, telling herself when she woke she'd find the energy to escape.

The headlights swung across the pale grey stone wall of another hairpin bend then up over the deserted mountainside. The lights of the last town shone below in the valley. Up here was solitude, and in winter, some of the best skiing Gennaro knew. For now though, the steep slope was covered in grass, the snow retreating to higher altitudes.

These mountains were as familiar to him as his city apartment. He'd grown up here. Learning to climb on the craggy bulk of jagged mountain looming straight ahead. Picking up a hammer and nails for the first time as he helped his uncle repair the ancient family home down in the valley. Kissing his first girl at a local summer celebration.

He slung a look at Chiara. She was still curled away from him, blocking him out even in sleep.

Pain jabbed his chest and his breath hissed as if from a puncture wound.

Had he been wrong to force her to come with him?

Had he just made the biggest mistake of his life?

No. You made that when you let pride get in the way of common sense. When you refused to explain and expected her simply to trust you.

Had it really been too much to ask?

His mouth twisted. Clearly it had.

He'd thought she knew him. That they'd built a relationship different from anything he'd ever shared with a woman.

He'd even started thinking about the future with Chiara! That was a complete first. One that had terrified as much as it excited him.

Rumour had it that permanency and the De Laurentis brothers didn't go together, at least as far as women were concerned. And yet he'd thought—

He shook his head, remembering Luca's teasing over the woman he'd kept so secret, so apart from the rest of his life.

But had Chiara felt the same? Clearly not.

One glitch. One tiny problem and suddenly she was rounding on him, accusing him of theft, of betrayal, attacking his honour.

When the chips were down, Miss High and Mighty Armati hadn't been able to forget the social gap between them. She'd rubbed his nose in it as if he were gutter trash instead of a proud man who'd built himself up from unassuming beginnings. As if he and his family couldn't be trusted because they were born poor.

That still lashed his pride. He'd never known such fury as when she'd flung those accusations.

He spun the wheel round another hairpin bend, taking it too fast then instinctively compensating, slowing the powerful car, his heart hammering.

This wasn't a road for careless driving. He'd seen too many accidents caused by people who believed testosterone equated to good driving skills.

Besides, he had Chiara with him. He couldn't risk hurting her.

A weight settled on his shoulders, stretching down his arms to his hands clenched tight on the wheel. He'd gambled outrageously tonight, staking his reputation on what some would call a wild scheme. That Chiara wouldn't storm into the nearest police station when it was all over and have him locked up for kidnap and coercion.

Not that any man in Italy would convict him.

But the potential repercussions might have stopped another man. Repercussions for his reputation, his business, and his brothers.

Gennaro hoped, for his family's sake, as well as his own, that he knew Chiara as well as he thought he did.

'We're here.'

Something brushed across her skin, a soft touch or a zephyr of air, and Chiara stirred.

'Time to get out,' the voice insisted and this time she jerked fully awake, her fogged brain recognising that deep, husky-edged voice.

Gennaro.

Shock and longing slammed her back in the seat and she opened her eyes to find him looming over her, the car door open. He reached out a hand and, for an instant, hovering on that brink between dream and reality, she almost took it.

Till she remembered.

'I may be just a spoiled blue-blood.' That acid taunt still jangled her nerves. 'And a mere fashion designer.' She lifted her chin and glared up into his shadowed face. 'But I'm perfectly capable of getting out of a car.'

Was that a hiss of indrawn breath? Surely not. It would take far more than that to land a blow on Gennaro De Laurentis and his overweening ego.

Finally he moved back. Chiara told herself she was pleased.

Then she looked past him and gasped.

She hadn't expected a city. She hadn't expected anything to rival Milan's best restaurant. But she had at least expected a town.

Not to be completely alone with her kidnapper.

Fear skipped down her backbone.

Above them, outlined against a sky scattered with bright stars, was a stunning building, its vast gabled windows glazed, presumably to catch the view. A single light burned inside, revealing a soaring space with beautiful timber ceilings, and nothing else. No furnishings. No people. No movement.

Alarm shot through her, drawing every nerve and sinew taut. Till she remembered he was watching her and forced her body to relax.

She refused to give him the pleasure of seeing

her crumble.

For one mad moment she considered grabbing the door, slamming it shut and throwing herself across into the driver's seat. But the manoeuvre wasn't for someone in a long dress and high heels. Gennaro would have the driver's door open before she could get there. And she'd bet he'd taken the precaution of removing the keys.

Chiara swung her legs out and stood carefully, feeling gravel shift under her feet.

A quick scan revealed that first look had been right. There was nothing but this sole building. Away in the valley to the left, pockets of distant lights revealed what must be the nearest habitation. Those might as well be on the moon for all the good they did her. The isolation unnerved her. Chiara was used to the constant hum of the big city, the vibrant sense of energy and bustle.

'This way.'

'Where are we?' She planted her feet and crossed her arms.

He sighed and turned. 'On my brother's property. A new resort I've just finished building for him.'

'Your brother?' Suspicion stirred.

'Yes, *that* brother. Luca, the one your Fabrizio is so scared of.'

'Scared?' She sneered. 'You've got to be kidding. Fabrizio is scared of no-one, much less a man who resorts to industrial espionage to succeed.'

She wasn't aware of Gennaro moving but suddenly his shoulders blocked the light from the building. She swallowed. If he was trying to intimidate he was doing a good job. Just as well she wasn't frightened of him. She tilted her head up and met that piercing scrutiny she felt rather than saw.

Her pulse hammered once, twice and then he moved back. 'If you want to stay out there with your pride, you're more than welcome. But it's more comfortable inside.'

He clicked the door lock on the car and strode off towards the resort. Leaving Chiara alone in the darkness. Cool air brushed her arms and shoulders and stirred the soft material of her full length skirt against her legs.

She spun around, surveying what she could of the site. The mountain rose behind the building and dropped down precipitously below them. The nearest village was far distant, too far to walk at night in these heels or barefoot, even if she trusted her night vision. The flat gravelled area was totally deserted. There was no other vehicle, nothing that looked like equipment left lying around. Nothing to help her break into the car so she could hot-wire it.

She snorted. As if she knew how to hot-wire a car. But she'd teach herself soon enough if given half a chance. Anything to get away.

Finally, reluctantly, she turned and walked towards the stream of light from the open door.

Gennaro might have the upper hand for now but she'd bide her time. Somehow she'd find an opportunity to escape. When she did, he wouldn't see her for dust.

Chapter Four

CHIARA'S FLESH PRICKLED WHEN SHE saw what awaited her inside the resort.

It wasn't quite as empty as she'd thought from outside.

On the other side of the enormous room, before a stone fireplace set in a wall of soaring glass, lay a large mattress. It was big enough for two.

Chiara's stomach twisted in a somersault that almost choked her. She blinked, breath stilling in her lungs as she took in the neatly folded blankets topped with a couple of pillows.

He couldn't think…

Stunned, she turned, noticing a rug spread across the wooden floor, complete with bright cushions and a massive picnic basket. There was also a bottle of wine in a beaten pewter ice bucket and a pair of elegant glasses.

If she didn't know better she'd think this the site of a romantic tryst, not a kidnap.

'All the luxuries of home,' she drawled, belatedly focusing on the overhead light. If there was electricity, were there also phones? Her phone was in her purse and as far as she knew it was still in the car.

Gennaro leaned back from the fire he was stoking then unfolded his long legs to stand. Even the enormous fireplace didn't dwarf him as he looked at her. The orange flames sent flickers and shadows into the room that emphasised the saturnine perfection of his dark features. That ultra-short, sculpted beard reinforced something she'd never seen in him till tonight. A ruthlessness, a hard edge that was about far more than the simple sex appeal she'd once revelled in.

He looked older, grimmer, more implacable than the laughing man she remembered from Rome.

Was it the surroundings or her overworked imagination that made him seem abruptly dangerous? And all too attractive. Disquiet filled her.

Chiara notched up her chin. Attack was surely the best defence. If he sensed any chink in her armour…

'Quite a little love nest you've got here.' She made herself stroll further into the room despite her churning stomach. 'If you have a taste for roughing it.' Once upon a time she'd have adored sharing an impromptu picnic by a blazing fire with him.

Except she wasn't that woman any longer. She couldn't afford to be.

She planted her hand on one outthrust hip in a challenging, sexy pose she'd seen so many models use. 'Sure I'm not intruding?' She made a production of peering towards the darkened doors leading off the back of the room. 'If you've got some poor, besotted woman here waiting for you I'm happy to take the car and drive somewhere a little more… up to my usual standards.'

Chiara cast a dismissive glance that hid her appreciation of the cosy scene. And her nausea at the thought of some other woman waiting to share intimacies with Gennaro.

The sound of slow clapping froze her to the spot.

'*Brava*. Spoken like a true society queen.' His deep voice brushed across her sensitised nerves. 'I should have known it was too much to expect a pampered aristocrat to appreciate a place like this. At least not till it's decked out with all the requisite luxuries.'

His barbed tone pricked. Absurdly, after all she'd been through, it made her blink and turn away.

Had he always thought that? Even when they'd been together? That she was nothing more than a rich, spoiled woman? That she couldn't appreciate the beauty of simple things?

What about the times they'd eaten, engrossed in each other and the rustic ambience of tiny, out of the way trattorias? The shared thrill of riding on his big, growling motorbike? The memorable picnic of bread, cheese and wine in a deserted olive grove? They'd made love beneath a gnarled, ancient tree with an intensity she could feel even now in the pit of her belly. She'd thought she'd died and gone to heaven.

Pressing a hand to her stomach, trying to keep in the ache of distress, Chiara swept a look around the space. It had vaulted wooden ceilings, high arching windows that would frame the views, and lots of exquisite detailing like the traditional carving on the door frames.

The undressed space, bare of furnishings, was spectacular, full of possibilities. Even the scent of fresh wood added depth and appeal.

'Who designed it?' Anything to change the subject.

'I did.'

Chiara swung around, eyebrows raised.

The look he sent her was pure challenge. As if he expected her to say something scathing. How could she? It was extraordinary. A perfect blend of modern and traditional design, with a unique twist that made it something special.

'Congratulations. You must be pleased.'

For an instant Gennaro's eyes widened then he frowned, his gaze narrowing on her. Clearly he hadn't expected that.

'What happens now?' She tried and failed not to dart a look at the mattress spread so invitingly beside the fire. Briskly she rubbed her arms, trying to counteract the sudden chill.

'It's just occurred to you to wonder about that?'

'No.' She stood straight, refusing to reveal how badly her nerves had frayed. 'I've been doing that ever since you abducted me.' She glared at him and drew a quick, sustaining breath. 'What I haven't worked out is how far you'll go to exact revenge for the fact I walked out on you.'

She'd thought Gennaro easy-going, laidback, except for his commitment to his work and the intensity with which he made love. Clearly she'd been mistaken.

'Revenge? You think that's what this is about?' His deep voice curled around her, stroking her flesh, reminding her he'd only ever had to touch her for her to fall into his arms.

Again her gaze skittered to the makeshift bed. Did she have it in her to resist him? Did she want to?

Fear at her own weakness hollowed her insides. She hated what he'd done to her. She hated that he'd snatched her tonight as easily as if she'd been some gullible kid. But if she was truthful, she didn't hate Gennaro De Laurentis nearly as much as she should.

'*Per la Madonna!* Stop looking like a scared virgin. I didn't bring you here to rape you!'

Chiara jutted her chin and suddenly the storm she'd been holding within burst free. She found herself stalking across the room towards him. She hadn't ever seriously thought Gennaro would stoop so low as sexual violence but she felt horribly shaky nevertheless. Tonight had rocked her to the core. She'd never felt so vulnerable in her life. First the auction and then being taken so easily, as if she wasn't a successful, competent woman, able to look after herself.

All her certainties, her self-confidence, wobbled and cracked under the pressure.

'Well, thank you for that assurance, Signor De Laurentis. It's good to know there are at least *some* boundaries you won't cross. I can't tell you how relieved that makes me feel.'

'Cut the sarcasm, Chiara, it doesn't suit you.'

'What? Pampered, worthless society princesses can't be sarcastic?'

'I didn't say you were worthless.' Indigo fire sizzled in his eyes.

'You implied it. You've done nothing but gripe at me all night. It's not my fault you've got a chip on your shoulder because you were born working class.'

'I don't have a chip—'

'You have one the size of a tree trunk. Why else would you harp on and on about my social standing?' She drew a shuddering breath, realising suddenly that she'd stormed up too close to him. The evocative scent of maleness, rich and enticing crept into her nostrils, reminding her how good it had felt to be naked with him.

Big hands clenched then flexed by his sides. Chiara swallowed hard, transfixed, wholly aware of the bed beside them. What was she thinking, pushing him like this?

Except when she was with him she found it hard to think. Especially when he wound her up like he had tonight. She didn't know whether it was anxiety or anticipation she felt at the idea she might push him too far.

With a muffled oath he turned away, striding across the room and slamming his hand against the wall.

'I hate it when you look at me like that,' he growled. 'Do you really think I'm going to hurt you?'

Everything in Chiara stilled as she registered something unfamiliar in his tone. If she didn't know better she'd think it was pain.

'I don't know what to think.' She shook her head, pushing away the hair that had come loose as she slept. 'I thought I knew you. But I was wrong.' Chiara swallowed convulsively, hating the vulnerability she heard in her voice.

He might not force her into his bed, but she had no confidence in her self-control. Not when the sight of him, the scent of his skin, even the tension radiating from his big frame spoke to her in primitive, unspoken ways that made her body soften and her blood rush eagerly. Beneath the tailored jacket beat the heart of a man who had more than a hint of wildness in his soul. A wildness that had always thrilled her.

It should be impossible, but just arguing with him turned her on.

She'd fought the realisation ever since she got in his car. How could she respond so to a man who'd betrayed her? How could she look at those clenched fists and imagine his long fingers sliding over her skin, rough to her smooth?

'Then know this, Chiara.' Suddenly he was before her, his stare pinioning her. She hadn't even heard him move. 'You have nothing to fear from me.'

Chiara bit her lip so hard it throbbed. He might not intend to hurt her. He might never touch her again, but she'd already discovered this man had the power to hurt her as no-one else could. Because he'd taken part of her heart.

She refused to let him take any more, no matter what ideas her weak body had.

'Good,' she snarled. 'Because if you did, my brother would kill you.' She shook her head, her hair swirling heavily around her shoulders, and planted her hands on her hips. 'No. *I* would kill you.'

She was sick of this. Sick not just of the regret and pain, but of the need he still stirred. It was as if Gennaro De Laurentis had got into her blood and nothing, not his lies or his scandalous behaviour tonight or even her common sense could eradicate him. Where were her hard won defences?

'That's more like it. That's the sassy woman I

remember.'

A slow smile tipped up one corner of Gennaro's mouth. To Chiara's amazement she read approval in his eyes. Approval and something else, something more intense, that made him suddenly look like a marauding buccaneer.

For a heartbeat, for two, she stood transfixed by the look on his face and by the answering thud of her heart.

'Right now this woman is hungry.' She spun away, needing to break free of that gleaming indigo gaze. It did things to her that were just plain wrong.

'You promised me dinner, Gennaro.' Chiara swallowed hard on his name. Once it had tripped so readily from her lips. 'All I can say is, after what you've put me through, this food had better be amazing.'

Gennaro leaned back on one arm, stretching his legs out, and watched Chiara through slitted eyes as she sat before the fire.

She was something else. The most vivacious, gorgeous woman he'd ever known. Even barefoot on a picnic rug, her legs tucked under her and her hair a long, ebony curtain around her shoulders, she had presence.

The flickering firelight chased shadows across her face, emphasising her sculpted cheekbones, the full curve of her lips and the neat angle of her jaw and pointed chin. Her eyes gleamed, sloe-dark and mysterious as she focused on the food he'd brought, just as if he wasn't there.

She reached for bread and bresaola, the distinctive cured beef his uncle made, adding rocket and a sliver of asiago cheese. Then she bit into the open sandwich with all the gusto of one of his labourers falling on food after a long day's work.

His gut clenched. Chiara was a woman with appetites and she didn't try to pretend they didn't exist. That was one of the things that had always appealed to him. Her innate honesty despite the fact she moved in such rarefied circles.

She was the only woman he'd dated who would tuck into pasta with enthusiasm, enjoying her food instead of calorie counting. More than once he'd found himself sitting back, watching her neat, precise bites, the eager way she tore at new-baked, crusty bread. The way she used all her senses, inhaling deeply and surveying each dish with approval before she ate. The way her eyes rolled in delight at some fantastic new flavour. That throaty little hum of approval that made his belly tighten.

Sharing that first meal with her was how he'd discovered she was a deeply sensual woman. As if it hadn't been obvious from the way she moved, touched, responded to her surroundings.

It had made him wonder too, what she did to burn off those calories, for despite the lush bounty of her breasts and the womanly curve of her hips, she was slender. His hands all but met around her waist. That was before he discovered she threw herself into life with a verve he'd never seen before. She didn't jog each morning, she *ran*. She didn't work at her designs, she lived and breathed them.

To his delight she was just as enthusiastic about sexual pleasure. The wholehearted way she'd given herself to him, the deliciously arousing way she'd responded to every caress, had been a revelation.

She'd demanded everything from him, but she'd given unstintingly too.

Heat drilled through his chest, dropping to eddy in his stomach and lower, tightening his groin.

Sex had always been phenomenal between them and he missed that.

He swigged a mouthful of crisp pinot grigio. But it did nothing to cool the flames licking inside.

Cavolo! It wasn't just the sex he missed. It was Chiara. Her smile, her rich laugh. The light in her eyes when she was happy. The way she leaned close as if gifting him with shared secrets when they spoke. Her zest for life and sense of humour. Even her pride when she spoke of her family.

He could relate to that. Wasn't his family the most important thing in his life?

Gennaro swallowed some more wine, feeling its cool track down into his chest.

Her family. If it weren't for her brother—

'What are you scowling about? If anyone has a right to scowl it's me. I'm the one who's been kidnapped.'

How the hell did she do that? She couldn't have noticed his expression because she hadn't deigned to look at him. Instead her attention was on a basket of fruit, fingers hovering over purple-black grapes and ripe peaches.

Gennaro imagined feeding her the rich, slippery peach flesh, tantalising her with it, licking the juice from the corner of her mouth, letting his—

'Gennaro?' Her voice was a sharp crack of sound.

'What?' Why did he let her distract him like that? He'd brought her here with a purpose. Instead he found himself brooding like a kid too long deprived of his favourite toy.

Chiara sighed and pushed away the food. 'Suddenly I've lost my appetite.' She reached for her glass and took a deep swallow.

It was a wine to be savoured and appreciated, one of his brother Aurelio's best. But she quaffed it as if seeking oblivion. That wasn't like her. Chiara was abstemious with alcohol, but she'd already downed two glasses of the fine wine as if it were water.

In the glow from the fire Gennaro saw the surface of her wine ripple.

Her hand was unsteady.

With nerves? He scowled, guilt ploughing through him.

He'd planned to force Chiara to face some home truths tonight and he'd revelled in the chance to crack her air of superiority. He knew it was her defence against importunate outsiders. He'd seen her don it before when people tried to get too close. But it galled him because he'd never expected her to use it on *him*.

Yet now, seeing her tremble, he hesitated.

She lifted her hand but this time she stifled a yawn. Perversely that rankled.

'Am I boring you?'

Her gaze slewed to his. 'Don't tell me, I'm supposed to hang on your every word. What's wrong? Have I dented your ego by concentrating on the food instead of you?'

Gennaro set his jaw. He'd always admired Chiara's spirit, but not when it was turned against him. He'd never let any woman get to him the way she did. She had a genius for it.

Or maybe it was because he still cared about her. 'Waspishness doesn't become you.'

'Surprise, surprise.' She waved her glass wide. 'You've already made your disapproval clear. And you know what? I really don't care.'

But her eyes shifted from his and for the first time since they'd arrived he felt real hope stir. She wasn't nearly as immune as she pretended.

She made a production of tucking her hair behind her ear, hiding another yawn in the process. Her eyes were heavy-lidded.

'You need sleep.' How could he be annoyed and impatient but at the same time protective? This woman tied him in knots.

She arched her brows in feigned surprise. 'You noticed.' She shook her head and her glossy hair slipped back around her face. 'It's not *my* choice to be sitting here in the middle of nowhere with you at this time of night.'

Gennaro watched her stiffen her shoulders as if preparing for battle and suddenly he felt the weight of weariness too. He was tired of fighting her. 'I didn't do it, you know.'

She froze. In the stillness he heard her sudden intake of breath.

'What didn't you do, Signor De Laurentis?' She gave him her best haughty look, a sure sign of defensiveness.

So it was Signor De Laurentis now.

How had they ever got to this? Gennaro still couldn't believe how suddenly, how completely, it had all gone wrong between them.

'I didn't betray your brother's plans to Luca. I didn't use the information you let slip about the palazzo he intended to buy.'

'You expect me to believe that?' She put her wine down on the hearth, the click of glass on stone loud. 'You expect me to believe that all the time it was really *me* you were interested in, not the fact my brother is your brother's biggest competitor? The fact that I was a potential goldmine of inside information on Fabrizio's plans to expand his business?'

Somehow she managed to look down her pert nose at him, as if, even sitting down, he wasn't half a head taller.

'Yes, I expect you to believe me. Why shouldn't you?'

Despite his determination to keep his cool, Gennaro felt once more the burn of indignation. He was a man of his word. A man of honour. In the early days honour was about all his family had. There'd been no surfeit of worldly riches to cushion them.

'Perhaps,' she murmured, staring back with all the hauteur of an empress surveying a slave, 'because you never bothered to say it before. Even when I all but begged you to deny it.'

Chapter Five

CHIARA HAD WAITED FOR HIM to tell her it wasn't true. That he hadn't turned over to his brother the one piece of commercially sensitive information she'd ever passed on. She'd felt horrified and guilty that she might have unwittingly betrayed Fabrizio.

If Gennaro had laughed off the idea when she'd confronted him in Rome she'd have believed him. But instead he'd stared at her stonily, refusing to allay her fears.

It was only then, watching the man she loved morph into a cold stranger, that she'd realised he'd not once given her any commitment. That for him their affair might be no more than a short term fling.

She'd tumbled in love with Gennaro so fast, so completely, but he…

It chilled her to discover that for all his passion, all his tenderness, she had no idea how he saw her, beyond a partner in pleasure.

And when she'd later learned from a friend that he'd engineered their first meeting, that he'd arranged to be introduced—

'My word should have been enough for you.' Gennaro's voice was stark.

Chiara's hackles rose, as they had that night weeks

ago. Time had marched on since the days when women blindly accepted what a man said without question. How dare he expect her not even to ask!

Yet, despite her fury, she couldn't drag her eyes away. She hated the way her heart beat quicker at the sight of him, lounging there in the firelight. He was the epitome of charismatic masculinity. Energy radiated from him. She felt it spark and tickle her skin.

His stunning eyes glinted beneath straight brows, his strong jaw set, and the firelight played on his dark brown hair, picking out the highlights of honey and caramel that had always intrigued her. With his mix of Latin and northern colouring he was the most beautiful man she'd ever known.

Beautiful on the outside. But it was the inside that mattered, wasn't it?

'Why should I take your word?'

He stared as if he'd never seen her before. 'Because you knew me. Because we were lovers,' he gritted out. 'You're not the sort of woman to give herself to a man she doesn't trust.'

He was right. That's what hurt the most.

Chiara arched an eyebrow. 'Lovers have been known to betray.'

Instantly his mouth twisted in a sneer and he sat straighter. 'Not a De Laurentis! Or is that too hard to believe because we don't come with the gilt-edged pedigree of the mighty Armati family?'

There it was again, that gripe about the social divide between their families.

'Oh, get over yourself, Gennaro. I'm not hung up on that stuff and you know it. If I had, would we have ever got together?'

He put his glass down and leaned towards her, all bunched muscles and taut strength. 'Perhaps I was a diversion. A bit of rough on the side. After all, when we met I didn't look like a man with money, just an ordinary builder.'

'A bit of rough?'

She didn't know whether to laugh or cry. As if there'd ever been anything ordinary about Gennaro.

He'd got off his big, growling bike and everything, from his height to his confidence, his easy stride and the hot, sensual awareness when their eyes met, had drawn her. Then he'd spoken and within minutes of being introduced by her girlfriend she'd known he was even hotter than his macho male exterior indicated, because he'd been charming, interesting and funny. He'd *listened*. He'd shared.

As for the dust of the building site on his boots – yes, it had been a change from glossy, hand-stitched loafers, but to have him accuse her of – what? Trawling for cheap sexual thrills?

Chiara shot to her feet, almost stumbling over the long dress wrapped around her legs.

'In that case, what was I?' Her breasts rose and fell as she struggled to drag in oxygen. She couldn't catch her breath. 'An amusement? A diversion? You think because I came from wealth I don't deserve basic respect? Is that why you thought it okay to rip my brother off? To use me?' She gagged on rising bile and swung away, unable to face him anymore.

When he looked at her did he really see no more than privilege and status, not a real woman?

A familiar ring tone pierced the heaving silence

and Chiara turned, spying her satin clutch purse in the shadows beyond the fireplace. How had she not seen it before?

Swift as thought she dived on it, wrenching it open and palming the phone.

'Fabrizio.' The call was from her brother.

Soon this nightmare would be over. With a gulp of relief she accepted the call, her mouth already forming the words that would bring help.

Except a big hand closed around hers, severing the connection, hauling the phone from her grasp.

'Hey! Give that back.' On tiptoe she leaned in, trying to reach it, but Gennaro swung it away out of her reach.

'Not yet. Not till we've sorted this out.'

He looked so superior, standing there staring down at her. So in control, while Chiara was a morass of jumbled feelings: anger, hurt and confusion.

'There's nothing to sort out. Now give me back my phone.' She made another swipe at it and missed. 'Or are you adding theft to your crimes?' She curled her lip. 'Abduction, false pretences, corporate espionage.'

'For the last time,' he snarled, 'I did *not* betray your brother's precious business plans.'

'Of *course* you didn't. You're just a paragon of virtue, aren't you, Gennaro?' She stuck one hand on her hip and held the other out. 'If you've got nothing to hide you'll give me my phone.'

'What, so you can call your dear brother? I think not.'

With one fluid movement he opened the full length glass window and stepped out onto the dark balcony. Chiara followed, was out the door when he raised his arm in a perfect arc and something flew through the darkness.

Chiara froze, unable to believe he had the gall to do it. Till somewhere in the distance she heard the sickening little crunch of her state-of-the-art phone smashing.

It was too much. She'd held onto her emotions, barely, through the nightmare of the auction, through abduction, through the craziness of finding herself alone in the wilderness with the man she hated. Or was it loved?

No, it couldn't be that. She wouldn't let it be.

She was exhausted and she'd never been so furious in her life. Anger welled up, burning white, to blind her, sear her lungs and shatter her defences.

Wildly she struck out, connecting with his chin in a glancing blow that probably hurt her more than him since he saw it coming and moved just in time.

'Chiara!'

What? Was she supposed to stand there and take whatever he dished out? Even in the gloom outdoors she could make out the surprise on his face. Presumably well-born women didn't know how to fight.

She stamped on his instep, wishing she was still wearing her stilettos then followed through with a vicious, jabbing knee to the groin. But he anticipated the move, jumping back and at the same time capturing her wrists. Chiara tried to wrench out of his hold but his hands were like manacles.

'Stop. You'll hurt yourself.'

Her laugh was brief and bitter. 'Not as much

as you've already hurt me.' She twisted hard, felt the burn of his hands against her wrists but still couldn't break his hold. A sob of frustration rose in her throat but she jammed her teeth shut, refusing to let the sound escape.

In a blur of movement Gennaro swung them around. She found herself backed against the cool, reinforced glass window, staring up into a face like a fallen angel's.

Her heart did that stupid little flutter and rage overflowed. At herself. At him.

'Let me go!' She aimed her knee up again but he evaded it then came in hard, pushing her up against the glass, his thighs imprisoning hers so she couldn't get purchase enough to attack.

'All my contacts were on there,' she gasped.

'You'll survive.' He grunted as she managed to jab an elbow to his ribs. He countered by pressing his full weight against her, splaying her against the wall of glass so she couldn't move.

'My *business* contacts. Or isn't that important since I'm a mere fashion designer?' She clawed at his hands, trying to sink her nails into flesh but apart from a smothered gasp it seemed to have no effect.

'You've got back-up.'

He was right, damn him. But that wasn't the point.

The point was she wanted to be far away from him. Somewhere safe where she couldn't look into his hard, proud face and wish it would soften just for her. Where she wouldn't feel the betraying pulse of heat between her legs or the imprint of his steel thighs against hers.

'I hate you, Gennaro De Laurentis. I've never despised anyone the way I do you. I never want to see you again.'

For endless moments he stared down at her. The firelight behind her flickered across features drawn tight and harsh. His nostrils flared, his lips thinning as if in pain.

'Then I've got nothing to lose, have I?'

Slowly, almost gently, he raised both her hands, till they touched the glass above her head. He shifted his grip, holding her wrists with just one hand, while the other slid down to her hair, stroking it from her cheek with a lingering caress that branded, dispelling any hint of chill from the night air.

Chiara dragged in a difficult breath, oxygen sawing into cramped lungs.

Indigo eyes clashed with hers. His mouth twisted. His warm breath was on her face, like coffee and spice. Behind him a thousand stars glittered in the dark sky, as if reminding her how utterly alone they were.

He shifted and she felt the movement right through her body. Then his hand slid lower, down her throat, over the light fabric of her bodice and she sighed.

She felt like she'd been waiting for his touch for an age.

His fingers skimmed the side of her breast, bare beneath the halter neck of her dress, as his mouth took hers.

Just like that the world exploded.

Chapter Six

GENNARO MEANT TO MAKE HER pay for the words that had cut so deep.

The thought of never seeing her again gouged a chasm in his soul. He'd spent weeks regretting that he'd let her walk out in high dudgeon. Too late he'd discovered that, with the help of her brother and his ultra-efficient bodyguards, she'd made it impossible to get near her again in Rome.

He didn't want to care the way he did. But he'd discovered, with Chiara, he couldn't switch off his feelings.

Or his body.

The feel of her soft curves cushioning him was too much to bear. Especially when her ragged breathing pushed those luscious breasts hard against him.

He shifted and she gasped as his erection nestled against her.

How could she be surprised? He only had to look at her and he was hard. Night after night alone in his empty bed had been torture. He'd let pride get in the way of what had been a perfect relationship.

Or had he let her believe the worst when he'd realised how much her distrust hurt? When he'd realised exactly how much he wanted her to believe in him.

His brother, Luca, reckoned he'd deliberately pushed Chiara away.

There'd be no pushing away now. The need in his belly and his groin couldn't be sated by anything other than Chiara, tight around him, screaming his name as she convulsed in his arms and he spilled himself inside her.

The thought was too much. He slammed his mouth on hers. No finesse, no gentleness, just hard, sure hunger.

Her mouth opened beneath his and there she was, lush peaches and wine, pure seduction, waiting for him. She gave a little purr of satisfaction in her throat and arched, rubbing her breasts against him.

Fire rocketed through his veins, shutting down his brain, shooting straight to his shaft, already surging hard against her soft belly.

Gennaro slipped his hand between them, cupped her breast, pinching the nipple in his fingers, and she released a low sound of pleasure in the back of her throat. He tasted it, swallowed it, then took her mouth harder, his tongue demanding. He couldn't get enough of the sweet taste of her. Like summer fruit and sex.

Always she'd done this to him. Right from the first.

He'd broken all the rules for her. Dating a woman he knew should be out of bounds because of the rivalry between their brothers. Begging an introduction from a friend. He, who didn't exert himself for any woman! Even rearranging his schedule to be in Rome more than he liked, just to be with her.

Her tongue slid against his. Between his spread legs her thighs shifted, trying to open, causing a friction that had him wondering if he'd last long enough to take her.

Gennaro shut his eyes, a groan escaping as she wriggled against him.

Spitfire one moment, seductress the next. What hope had he?

He tweaked her nipple and she groaned. 'More.' He felt the word in his mouth, rather than heard it.

An instant later he was using both hands to scrabble her long skirt up. He almost swore when her hand got in the way, till he realised she was trying to help him. Together they hauled the flame red material higher and higher till there was silky, naked skin beneath his fingers. She was smooth and enticing and he wanted to lose himself in her.

In one swift move he hoisted her high, pinned against the glass, so he had unfettered access. Her heat was against his crotch, her slender legs about his waist. And before him, the delicious bounty of her breasts.

'Undo the dress if you don't want it torn.' He didn't recognise the voice but it must be his because he felt the harsh rasp on his throat.

Arms raised, she did something behind her neck and the fabric fell, revealing pert, beautiful breasts, their dusky nipples begging for attention.

Then he was tasting her, laving her breast, sucking hard while his hand took the weight of the other one.

Chiara grabbed his head, hauling him close, burying him against her, her fingers hard against his ears.

Gennaro thought he could stay like this forever, the sound of her hungry gasps loud in his ears, her sensuous body moving against him. Except for the burning in his groin.

She rocked against him, her hands clutching, her flesh hot against his face and suddenly he heard that familiar gasp of astonishment. Just as if she'd never come in his arms before. Every time it enchanted him, made him want to pleasure her over and over again.

He tugged her nipple harder into his mouth, sliding one hand down to where she burned like a furnace against his erection. Her silk panties were wet. He pressed his thumb hard and she writhed, shouting his name.

On and on it went, as if the climax had been years building, not mere weeks.

But Gennaro understood. He was the same. If he could unzip his trousers without coming it would be a miracle. She was so hot and alluring. Irresistible.

His hands were unsteady, his fingers fumbling. But eventually he managed to undo his trousers, rip aside the fabric. One quick tug and her underwear fell away, torn through.

'Gennaro.' It was a sweet whisper but it was the final confirmation he needed to be absolutely sure. One hard thrust and he was there, right up to the heart of her, surrounded by silken heat and the final reverberations of her orgasm.

Her fingers dug into his shoulders and her legs tightened around him as if to keep him close.

Like he was going anywhere!

He looked into her face, unreadable in the scant light. But he could make out the gleam of her eyes as she watched him. He heard her laboured gasps, felt her rock her pelvis against him.

Then it was upon him, an unstoppable force, making him surge against her, striving for a place only she could take him. The night was silk and darkness and tight, rhythmic throbbing. It was peaches and wine and hot woman. It was pleasure so sharp, so deep it teetered on the brink of pain.

And, finally, it was white hot light and rapture burning him alive as ecstasy consumed him, consumed them both. Their cries were raw and shocked.

Gennaro surrendered to delight, knowing nothing ever had surpassed the sheer intensity of this moment.

Chapter Seven

CHIARA CLUNG TO GENNARO, HER body in lockdown after the most cataclysmic orgasm of her life.

He stumbled back inside and collapsed onto the mattress. Even his sudden weight on her, forcing the last air from her lungs, couldn't rouse her. She'd died and gone somewhere else. Somewhere bliss reigned.

Her bones had dissolved so that when Gennaro rolled onto his back she simply went with him, tight in his embrace.

It wasn't just her bones that had dissolved. It was her brain too. That realisation came slowly, as the flush of arousal finally died and something like normality returned.

Except what was normal? Her wildly mixed emotions *before*? Or this luxurious lethargy, this sense of completion and more, of rightness, as she lay with Gennaro?

His breathing was harsh, tickling the hair on her forehead. His heart pounded beneath her ear, matching the beat of hers.

As if they were still together, joined as one.

Dismay pierced her, a sharp stab to the ribs, dragging the air from her lungs.

What had she done? She'd told herself she was

finished letting him make a fool of her. Yet one touch, one kiss and she'd gone up in flames.

'Chiara? Are you all right?' The sound of his voice, that husky post-coital rumble she knew so well, exacerbated her distress.

She rolled away, flinging herself out of his arms, scrambling to find purchase with hands and legs that wouldn't coordinate. She needed to get off this bed and—

'Oh, no, you don't.' Firm fingers gripped her upper arm.

His touch made her frantic. She had to get away. Clear her head. Think. She couldn't think with him touching her. She didn't trust herself.

Despite his grip she slithered to the edge of the mattress. She was almost there, almost touching the floor, when a solid weight pinned her to the bed, crushing her.

A solid, hot weight.

Gennaro, lying over her, encompassing her.

For an instant panic struck and she thought she couldn't breathe, then she realised he must be propping himself over her so she didn't take his full weight.

'You're not running away from me now. Not yet. Not till we've talked.'

'Talked? Is that what you call it?' She tried to sneer but it emerged as a gasp.

To make things worse, despite the clothes they still half-wore, there was far too much skin to skin contact. His trousers must be around his ankles for she felt the strong, hairy length of his legs against hers. Worse, her dress was rucked up around her waist and her bare backside cradled his groin.

Chiara bit her lip as she felt him stiffen and grow. She pressed her pelvis down into the mattress to avoid the intimate contact but he merely shifted his slick weight over her.

He said something under his breath. Something soft yet pithy. Chiara moved and heard the break in his breathing, felt the tension in the body blanketing hers. She stilled, telling herself she didn't want this.

Pity she didn't believe it.

'I want to talk to you, Chiara.' He sounded strangled. 'But you have to promise not to run.' His lips were against her ear, a caress that remarkably was just as arousing as the feel of his erection against her naked buttocks and his iron-hard thighs capturing hers.

'Why? Because you *bought* me?'

'Because we have things to discuss.'

She shook her head. 'No. I tried talking to you before, remember? I begged you to explain.' That still rankled. More, it tore a gaping hole in her heart that she'd had to plead with the man she loved and still he'd been unmoving, unwilling to explain.

'You're not leaving till we've had this out.'

'You're an arrogant bully, Gennaro.'

'But you still want me.' Slowly he slid his length, hot and solid, against her flesh and a quiver of arousal shot through her. Chiara squeezed her eyes shut. She shouldn't want him. She shouldn't.

A hand insinuated itself under her hip bone then down, covering her mound. One finger found her clitoris, circling with intent, and the fires that had burned to cinders suddenly reignited.

'Oh, yes, you want me,' he gloated as her pelvis

tilted into his touch. 'You're just scared to admit it. Scared to face the truth.'

The fact he was right didn't help. Chiara's breath came in little pants as he pressed against her from both the front and the back, teasing, tempting her.

'I'm not scared of you.' Her voice was thin and far too high, a mere wisp of sound, but it was the best she could do.

'Prove it then.'

Suddenly, remarkably, he was gone. She lay, gasping and shivering on the mattress, a waft of cool evening air brushing her bare skin. Yet the imprint of his touch lingered. She felt… unfinished, needy.

Damn the man! What had he done to her? Had he cast some spell so she couldn't even walk away and stay away?

She lifted herself on her hands and there he was beside her, lying on his back, arms behind his head, eyes dark as the sky just after sunset, watching her.

'Go on then, Chiara. Prove you're not scared of me. Take what you want instead of pretending this doesn't exist between us.'

How any man could look so arrogant lying there in a jacket and shirt, with his trousers around his ankles she didn't know. But Gennaro achieved it. It wasn't just because of that imposing erection. It was more. That fearless, challenging look. The nonchalance of his arms behind his head. The very stillness of him.

She should take her chance and go.

She should walk away.

But he was right. She wanted him. Again. Still. *Always.*

The curse of it was she didn't just want his body.

She wanted his love. How pathetic was that?

She set her jaw. No way was she giving him the satisfaction of knowing. But, she discovered, leaving him now was impossible.

Holding his gaze she got to her knees, gripped the bunched skirt of her dress and with a swift upward movement, drew her dress, her precious new design, up and over her head, flinging it in an arc of red silk chiffon into the shadows.

Gennaro made a sound deep in his throat. A raw sound of approval that made her chin lift. His eyes glowed, hot and needy and his erection stirred. He shifted restlessly.

For a whole minute Chiara knelt, holding his gaze, feeling her feminine power run strong within. He might have bought her and forced her here. He might be bigger and stronger, and damn him, he might still hold a place in her heart, but he was at her mercy too. Her nakedness gave her strength.

He swallowed hard, his gaze dipping to her breasts and she felt them tighten to throbbing buds, eager for his touch. The pulse between her legs pounded insistently.

Slowly, oh so slowly, she made her way to him. Despite his relaxed pose his muscles were bunched, tension rising from him like a force field.

Chiara smiled as she straddled him. Not where he wanted, but close enough to tease. Then, still holding him with a look she reached down to his shirt. With one almighty tug she ripped the two sides apart, buttons splattering the floor. She shoved aside the fine weave cotton and splayed her hands over his hot flesh, like damp satin against her palms.

Bending, she drew in his spicy scent, nuzzled

him, feeling his heart hammering against his ribs. Slowly she licked, tasting salt and man, deliciously familiar. She stopped, flooded by remembrance, then forced the memory aside, determined to concentrate on the present.

She sucked his nipple into her mouth and he bucked beneath her, his breath sharp. Yet still he kept his hands anchored behind his head, as if giving her permission to take control.

Slowly she explored his torso, kissing, nipping, licking. Letting her nipples swing and slide against him, feeling every jerk and indrawn breath as he fought not to respond. But his eyes closed and his brow creased in a frown of pain from holding back. His mouth was tight, his jaw locked, only the throbbing pulse at his throat moving.

She kissed lower, to his navel, his hip bone, and his erection surged higher. Needy. She ignored it. He didn't deserve that. Not after what he'd done to her. Instead she rose on all fours to trail her tongue along the seam of his lips. Instantly they opened and he lifted his head, kissing her back. The unfamiliar brush of his soft beard teased.

Chiara retreated. She didn't want his kiss. It made her lose her mind. Already her body ached at the emptiness within. She was wet and pulsing with need for him. That was enough. That was more than enough.

This was *her* choice. Her pleasure.

Dimly it struck her that it would be fine payback if she got up and left Gennaro now. But she couldn't do it. She wanted him too much.

Grabbing his shaft she eased herself down, pausing for a delicious moment of anticipation. Then she bore down steadily till they were hip to hip and she felt him high inside her, big and powerful and just perfect. Pleasure radiated through her.

The moment strained against time. Her breath held and so did his.

But she couldn't sustain it. The need to move was too strong. Chiara raised herself and found slitted indigo eyes watching her. That look seared deep, right to her soul, and she faltered.

When she found her rhythm again it was to discover he no longer lay passive. His hips moved to the beat of pleasure she'd created. She was glad, for no matter what she'd told herself, this had always been about *them*.

Hurt lanced at the realisation there was no them. Not anymore. Between them they'd destroyed the trust and hope they'd once had.

'Chiara? *Tesoro*. What is it?'

'Nothing.' She planted her hands on his shoulders as she rose then fell again onto him, her eyelids drifting low at how good they felt together.

This would be the last time.

Suddenly his hands were on her hips, urging her on.

'Come to me.' His voice was gravel and suede and so seductive. Despite her earlier determination, she found herself leaning down as he arched up to take one nipple in his mouth. He sucked hard as he powered up and her slick, hot flesh slid against him. Another surge of movement and another and Chiara couldn't hold back. Those easy, deliberate moves became abrupt, uncoordinated. But he held her through them, giving her what she needed, caressing her breast.

Then came a roaring, blinding flash of heat that rolled on and on. Or maybe the roar was from Gennaro, pumping hard and recklessly within her. She felt his breath against her breast and he came like a force of nature, tumbling her back into ecstasy just as she'd climbed the heights and thought it was all over.

But it wasn't over. It would never be over.

Their hearts pounded in unison and they trembled together. He wrapped his arms around her slumped, sated body, cradling her as if she was utterly precious.

The last thing she remembered was the hot track of a single tear, running down the side of her nose to her mouth.

Chapter Eight

DAWN LIGHT BATHED THE ROOM when Chiara woke. She was curled beneath a blanket, spooned up against Gennaro, his naked warmth against her back and legs. At her nape she felt the gentle exhalation of his breath.

She felt… just right.

Wide-eyed, she stared out the window, watching the flush of colour across the vista of remarkable saw-toothed peaks. It was a perfect morning, clear, not a cloud to be seen, as if the world was new and fresh.

The snow caps turned gold and peach, the shadows in the folds of the mountains deep indigo. The colour of Gennaro's eyes.

Her heart squeezed and her breathing faltered.

She'd thought herself free of him but a single night, less, a few hours, had cured her of that deception.

Even her volcanic rage at his manipulation hadn't kept her safe. It wasn't just that she still wanted him sexually, though the depth of that need had shattered her. It was that she cared for him. Cared what he thought of her. Cared enough to wake with a heart at once elated by last night and bruised by the reality of what must follow.

Chiara lay unmoving, watching the sunlight

creep higher, washing the mighty Dolomites in colour, wishing the sunlight could wash away the darkness between her and Gennaro.

But last night had solved nothing. If anything it had highlighted her weakness. She'd kept Gennaro at bay in Rome with the help of a heavy schedule and her brother's security team. But one meeting and she'd fallen for Gennaro again like a ripe plum, despite her protests.

Which left her where, precisely?

She shivered, then stilled, fearing she'd wake him. Her mind was such a mess she needed to be alone to sort out what to do. All she knew with certainty was that she couldn't stay here. Her feelings were too close to the surface. She felt too vulnerable, and too needy.

Carefully she sidled off the mattress, holding her breath till the blanket Gennaro had pulled over them in the night settled and she saw he hadn't moved.

She padded across the floor, picking up her crumpled dress and lifting it over her head. It slithered down over sensitised skin like an echo of last night's arousal. She didn't have any underwear, just the dress. She'd heard her panties tear when he ripped them away on the balcony. She wouldn't waste her time searching for them.

Yet she lingered, looking at him. His hair tousled dark chocolate with hints of caramel. His nose strong, his lips sensuous, even in sleep. His broad shoulders looked powerful against the softness of the bed and she thought of how he'd held back, letting her set the pace and take what she wanted as she rode him last night.

No. It didn't mean anything. It was just sex.

It hurt to think that might be the only real thing they'd ever had between them. At this moment she had no idea if she believed he'd betrayed her or not. But the things he'd said, the hurt he'd inflicted…

Swiftly she scooped up her discarded shoes and her bag, then tiptoed to his trousers, discarded in the night. As she suspected, his keys were in his pocket. Her fingers closed around them and she told herself this was what she wanted. The chance to escape.

Chiara refused to let herself consider why she didn't feel triumphant as she left the building and crossed the gravel drive. It wasn't that she'd forgiven him for kidnapping her. But her fury had softened. Things didn't seem as simply black and white as they had last night.

The early morning chill and the rough surface beneath her feet were reminders of reality, shredding the haze of wellbeing that had encompassed her as she woke.

She flung her shoes onto the back seat. If she was driving this monster car, so much more powerful than her little city runabout, she wouldn't hamper herself with heels.

Even then she took a moment to draw in a deep breath. It was scented with the mountains – earthy with a note of sweetness from the flowers strewn across the silvery green grass. The nearest stand of trees was down below. Up here the air was crisp and clear and heady.

She swung her gaze back to the resort. It really was perfect in this setting, a beautiful design. But her eyes were on the vast expanse of glass in the room where Gennaro lay. How long before he woke? What if he saw her now and—

No. Imagining things had changed was pointless.

Chiara slid into the car, buckled her seatbelt and surveyed the controls. Surely this couldn't be too hard. She'd seen her brother drive a manual car often enough. Clutch, brake and accelerator. Foot on the clutch while she started the ignition.

The air splintered as the car roared like a vengeful dragon woken out of hibernation. Chiara started, her hands damp and pulse fast as she eased back on the accelerator, worked the handbrake and there, she was moving. Shooting forward rather than moving slowly. The car jumped and she remembered to work the clutch.

Pulse pounding, she brought the car to a halt at the lip of the slope. Her heart rose in her throat as she surveyed the sweep of road, a series of hairpin bends looping down and down to the valley below. In this unfamiliar car-

But she'd had her licence for years. And she knew the principles of driving a manual. She'd be fine.

Lifting her foot off the brake, she nosed the low-slung car down the first slope, eyes glued to the snaking curve just ahead.

Gennaro woke to the throaty growl of an engine. And to the realisation he was alone. Snapping his eyes open, he jerked up, scanning the room. No Chiara. No dress. No shoes.

And from the forecourt that grumbling roar.

He leapt from the bed.

His sports car, all that streamlined, lethal power,

was juddering in response to inexpert handling. Worse, it was heading for the road.

His heart lurched sickeningly. Was Chiara so desperate to get away, she'd risk her neck in a car she couldn't drive? On that of all roads?

In an instant he was out on the balcony, shouting her name. But the engine drowned his voice. Desperation and fear clawed at him.

Spinning on one foot he raced inside, scooping up trousers on his way out the door.

He had to stop her.

Chiara's hands stuck to the wheel, her fingers stiff and aching from the stress of bringing the super car down the mountain. The road was smooth and paved but those curves were treacherous for someone struggling to control this powerful engine.

There'd been one heart-in-mouth moment when her wheels had slid in the gravel at the side of the road, above the precipitous drop. She'd thought it would be the end of her.

But she'd managed. She was doing it!

Already she was halfway down to the valley. Soon she'd be back in civilisation. She could return to her own world. To the city, her friends, her busy schedule.

So why was her heart like a lead weight in her chest?

She should be triumphant. She'd engineered her own rescue. She'd escaped Gennaro and his abduction. She'd proven she was no easy victim.

Chiara jammed her foot on the brake, felt the big car buck and belatedly remembered the clutch.

With a shaking hand she switched off the ignition and set the handbrake. The sudden silence was
loud after the throb of the engine.

Just ahead the first stand of trees, dark and imposing, stirred in the slight breeze. Overhead a lone
bird soared. Below in the valley she saw sunlight
glint on a moving car heading out of a tiny village
of old-style wooden houses.

She told herself she should move off the road.
But there was no pull-over spot. Besides, the road
seemed just for the unfinished resort. There was
no traffic.

Her mind busied itself with all those thoughts,
but no matter how she tried Chiara couldn't block
the one, nagging idea that had stopped her in her
tracks.

She was running. Again.

Wasn't that what Gennaro had accused her of
last night?

Wasn't that what she'd done in Rome when she'd
confronted him and he'd refused even to discuss
the possibility he'd passed on information about
Fabrizio's plans to his brother?

It was definitely what she'd done when she'd
refused to take Gennaro's calls or open his messages. When, for the first time ever, she'd used her
brother's professional security team to isolate her
from any contact.

She sagged back in her seat, dragging shaking
hands from the wheel.

Lately she'd felt like a prisoner, hemmed in by
the protection she'd used to keep her safe from
Gennaro's attempts to see her. It was only yesterday,
travelling alone to Milan, that she'd felt for the first

time free, like herself again.

It said something that she'd taken such steps to hide herself, didn't it?

What was she scared of?

Being hurt even more than she had been? It didn't seem possible.

She swallowed hard, the movement a convulsive grating as if over shattered glass.

She was scared to admit she'd fallen in love with Gennaro De Laurentis and that even the possibility he'd used her hadn't destroyed her feelings.

I didn't do it, you know.

Last night, for the first time, he'd denied betraying her confidence, betraying her.

Her heart had leapt at his words but she'd refused to soften. If he'd been innocent then he would have told her all those weeks ago. An innocent man would.

And yet…

She shook her head, unable to marshal her whirling thoughts. She didn't know what to believe, what to think. All she knew was that she felt like her heart was breaking all over again. Because she'd turned her back on him, running at the first chance she'd got.

It was time she stopped running. Time to confront Gennaro and have this out once and for all. Even if she came out emotionally bruised, at least she'd know she'd done everything she could.

Setting her teeth, Chiara reached for the ignition. How she'd turn this car around and back up the mountain she didn't know exactly. But she'd find a way.

Movement caught her eye. A tumbling dark mass

hurtling down the grassy slope above her. She just had time to register the fact when it, *he*, was on the road, slamming into the parked car.

'Gennaro?' Chiara wrenched open the door, then remembered she still wore a seatbelt. The catch almost defeated her damp, clumsy hands but finally she was free, stumbling out the door.

Hard hands grabbed her and tugged her against an even harder, hot body. He was panting, his heart hammering. His torso was bare and slick with sweat and yet she'd never wanted to be anywhere as much as she wanted to be here in the sunlight in the arms of the man she loved.

Did that make her weak?

She didn't care. She was where she belonged.

'Are you all right?' She could feel him shaking all over, yet he stood tall, his arms around her, locking her to him. He wore trousers but no shirt and she pressed closer, revelling in his embrace.

'Should be asking you that,' he gasped, his breath ruffling her hair, his chest rising and falling with the force of a massive piston.

'I'm fine.'

'Sure? That car…' His hands ran up and down her back as if checking for injuries.

Chiara didn't move. Instead she inhaled the scent of him, all hot, masculine spice and sunshine.

He shifted and toes touched hers. She looked down.

'You're barefoot?' Not just barefoot but bleeding. Scratches crisscrossed his instep.

'No time for shoes.' Still his chest worked like bellows. No wonder, since he'd sprinted downhill, shortcutting the car.

Chiara shook her head. The slope was ridiculously steep. 'Have you got a death wish? You could have been killed, racing down here like that.'

She reared back as much as she could in his iron hold. His hair was rumpled, his nostrils flared. There was a graze along one cheek and another over his collarbone. 'Let me look at you.'

He didn't shift or loosen his hold.

'Gennaro! You're injured. Let me see.'

One corner of his mouth curled up. 'You care.'

'Of course I care!' She'd never stopped caring, even when she hated him. 'Now let me look at you. Have you got a first aid kit in this rocket of yours?'

'Rocket?' His smile grew and Chiara felt something vital melt inside. 'Not with you driving. That's the only reason I managed to catch you.'

'Why did you?' Suddenly the sense of lightness faded. She slammed into reality with a thump. 'You thought I'd crash the car and you didn't want my death on your conscience?'

When he'd shot down the mountain, ignoring the danger, hope had soared. For surely only a man who cared would be so reckless of his own neck. But what if she was wrong?

His hand brushed the hair from her cheek then lingered, stroking. His eyes darkened, holding hers captive.

'I've never been so frightened in my life as watching you drive away.'

'I'm a good driver!'

'Yes.' His look was sombre. 'But you've got no experience of a car like this, or these roads. And you were upset.' He paused. 'That was my fault. I shouldn't have done what I did.'

There was something in his voice she hadn't heard before. Could this be the same man who'd frozen her out when she'd sought reassurance in Rome?

'What? You shouldn't have made love to me?' Despite what she'd said last night about it being just sex, it had felt like making love. It always had, with Gennaro.

'Never that, *tesoro*.' His thumb stroked her mouth and a pulse of awareness passed between them. She pressed her hands to his chest, revelling in his strength.

He drew a mighty breath. 'I shouldn't have forced you to come with me. I scared you and, stupid as it seems to admit it now, I hadn't thought about that in all my clever planning.'

'I shouldn't have tried to cut you out of my life the way I did.'

His dark eyebrows soared.

She shrugged. 'You're not the only one with regrets.' She hesitated then went on in a rush. 'That's why I stopped the car. I realised I needed to come back and… talk.'

He looked down at her as if she spoke a foreign language. 'Talk?'

'Yes, talk. I was about to turn the car around and head back up to the resort.'

Chiara couldn't remember ever seeing Gennaro at a loss for words. He might consider himself a simple builder at heart, despite his commercial success, but he had charm and easy confidence in abundance. He could wrap any woman around his little finger.

'You were going to *turn* the car? *Here*?' He surveyed the road, the blind curve ahead, the minimal space, and grew pale. 'That settles it,' he said finally. 'I'm driving.'

She nodded, ignoring the way her pulse knocked at the prospect of them finally talking this out. This could be the last time she saw him. She forced herself to sound matter of fact. 'Okay. As soon as we're back at the resort I'll check your injuries.'

'No. Not there. Down to the town.'

Chiara frowned. 'Why?' He'd gone to all this trouble to get her alone. Kidnapping her! Now he wanted to take her into a town?

'I did wrong last night. Abducting you, bringing you all the way up here, so you felt vulnerable, in my power. I shouldn't have done it.'

Perversely there was a tiny part of her that had revelled in the sheer outrageousness of his actions. A part of her that had thrilled to his desperate need to get her to himself.

'We're going to talk this through. Sensibly and properly. But somewhere you're comfortable. With other people, a phone if you want it.'

He was handing her the power to leave him if she chose. She read determination and something that looked like fear in his expression. Her silly heart tumbled over and she put her hand in his.

'So long as there's decent coffee too.'

Chapter Nine

CHIARA SLIPPED INTO THE SEAT opposite Gennaro, feeling self-conscious.

In jeans and a melon-coloured cotton sweater she was perfectly respectable, albeit far more casual that usual. She'd been grateful for the change of clothes, and the soft leather flats with their cute bows were a relief after her stilettos.

She looked fine. She fitted right in at this pleasant, little outdoor café. She tilted her chin up, drinking in the warmth of the sun, trying to reinstate her usual air of unconcern.

Yet she still felt that faint burning blush. She'd worn it ever since Gennaro persuaded the owner of the small boutique around the corner to open early so she could buy some clothes.

Chiara had stood there as the woman's sweeping gaze took in not just Chiara's rumpled evening wear, but Gennaro's bare chest and feet. He'd looked raffish and outrageously handsome and utterly unconcerned, charming the woman with that devastating grin. Then the woman had shaken her head, tsked and smiled and said something in that incomprehensible local dialect as she opened the doors and waved Chiara inside.

Now, fully clothed, even with new underwear – the heat in her cheeks deepened, remembering the boutique owner's silently arched brows at that purchase – she was ready to face Gennaro.

But the way he watched her was too unsettling. It made the nerves in her stomach swoop and circle like eagles riding the mountain thermals.

'What? Why are you staring?' Chiara sat straighter, trying not to gawk back at the man who, in a newly acquired dark blue T-shirt, looked rough-hewn and gorgeous. He stole her breath.

'You're so beautiful.' He leaned over and took her hand, lifting it to his mouth and pressing a kiss to her palm that sent shivery delight right through her. 'I want to eat you all up,' he murmured, his breath a hot haze on her flesh. 'The question is where to begin.' His eyes glinted and Chiara felt herself melt.

He did it so easily, distracting her. But she couldn't afford to let him this time. This time they had to *talk*.

She tugged her hand free, ignoring Gennaro's frown, just as the waiter came with the coffee Gennaro had ordered.

To break the intensity of the moment she sipped her coffee and leaned back in her chair. 'Perfect. Strong and sweet. You remembered.'

'Of course. I remember everything about you.'

Her eyes snapped to his.

Gone was his teasing humour. Suddenly Gennaro looked more sombre than she'd ever seen him. In the daylight tiny lines fanned the corners of his eyes and there were grooves etched around his mouth. He looked hard and a little fierce and – worried?

He didn't look at all like the arrogant man who'd

kidnapped her or seduced her into pleasure just a few hours ago.

He looked tired, she realised. And tense.

'You didn't do it, did you?'

He met her stare with an unblinking look.

'The information I let slip about Fabrizio finding a rundown palazzo perfect for refurbishment as a luxury hotel. You didn't tell your brother the details, did you?'

'How do you know?' His eyes gave nothing away, yet she knew in her bones she was right.

She slumped back in her seat, suddenly exhausted. 'You told me. Last night, remember?'

Why hadn't she listened then? Because she'd been too caught up in righteous indignation to listen?

'Does it make a difference what I say?'

'Of course it does.' She put her cup down with a click, but cradled it in her hands, as if its warmth could counteract the chill filling her.

One sleek dark eyebrow rose. 'Are you saying you believe me? The man you walked out on? The man who abducted you?'

There was no sneer in his expression. Just curiosity. She was grateful for that.

'Last night you said you hated me.' His voice dropped to a pitch that made her belly squeeze. Was that pain she heard?

'Last night I was lashing out. Besides, you deserved it.'

Gennaro held her gaze then nodded slowly. 'I did. I shouldn't have put you through that.' His face looked drawn. 'When I realised I'd made you so desperate you'd take your life in your hands in my car…'

Chiara found herself leaning forward, her hand on his forearm. It was strong and sinewy, warm, and the hairs tickled her palm. He felt real and solid.

She didn't want to let him go.

'I wasn't in any danger.' Well, not too much. 'And it was my own fault for racing off rather than facing you.' Chiara swallowed. 'I was a coward.' She stopped, choking down pain. 'Again. I ran from you before.'

'I don't blame you.'

Stunned, she lifted her head.

'I behaved like a lout. A self-absorbed kid, demanding that you trust me without even bothering to deny the allegation.'

Chiara frowned.

Gennaro closed his hand over hers, sandwiching it between his warm flesh. 'My brother Luca says the way I behaved towards you—'

'You've spoken to him about me?'

'Of course. I needed to find out what had happened.' He paused, his expression unusually sombre. 'Luca thinks I behaved badly.' Gennaro's mouth tilted in a twisted smile. 'That's the polite version.'

'Your *brother* thinks that?'

Despite his stern features, Gennaro's eyes twinkled. 'He's not the antichrist, you know. He's a decent man and a clever one, despite being your brother's arch rival. And I can tell you he was furious I'd let you walk out the door believing the De Laurentis family engaged in industrial espionage.'

Gennaro's rueful expression made her wonder exactly what his brother had said. But that wasn't the point. The point was he'd just confirmed again that he was innocent.

'But why *did* you?' She leaned forward, as if proximity would help her understand. 'You must have known I'd believe you if you denied it.'

'Must I?' He sighed and dropped his gaze to their joined hands, to the spot where his thumb stroked hers, eliciting a new sort of tension in her body.

He looked so miserable, so unlike his usual assured self, she felt something inside her crumble.

'Yes. You must.' Chiara stopped, then realised that again she was playing safe. Playing the coward. Until these last three weeks she'd have said she was strong, resourceful and yes, brave, when she needed to be. At least she'd been that while pursuing her career. But in her private life it was another matter.

She drew herself up. 'I love you, Gennaro.'

At her softly spoken words his eyes widened and he sat straighter, his grip on her hand hard. He opened his mouth to speak but she stopped him.

'No. Let me finish. If I don't get this out now I might never do it.' She bit her lips when they began to tremble. This felt too much like walking on a tightrope between two mountain peaks. With a rising wind buffeting her. 'I've never been in love before and I was caught up in the excitement of it.'

Gennaro's eyes glinted and she tried not to wonder if he'd shared that feeling.

'I'd hoped you might begin to feel the same about me but I didn't know how to find out. Not without laying myself bare by telling you how I felt. And I'd learned to be cautious.' She hesitated, wondering how to explain. 'You were right about Fabrizio and me coming from a different world to you. But it's not all champagne and caviar. We both learned early that a lot of people are only interested in us because of the family name, our money or supposed power.'

'Someone hurt you.' It was a low growl that lifted the hairs at her nape. It sounded like he wanted to damage whoever had done that. The notion gave her hope, she felt it tremble into life deep inside.

She shrugged stiffly. 'It was a long time ago and it taught me not to judge at face value.'

She watched him digest her words.

'Fabrizio was complaining that maybe he had a mole in his office, since your brother pipped him at the post on the deal he'd been secretly planning for months. My ears pricked up when I realised he was talking about the old palazzo I'd told you about just the week before.'

She drew a slow breath. 'And especially when I learned the name of the rival who'd sneaked in that last minute higher bid – Luca De Laurentis.' She fixed him with a steady stare. 'I felt so *guilty*. I didn't want to believe you'd betrayed me. But you hadn't told me your brother and mine were rivals.'

'Would you have gone out with me if you'd known?'

'You've got to be kidding.' Chiara huffed an outraged breath. 'Blood might be thicker than water but my brother's business doesn't dictate my personal life. At least not till now.'

Gennaro leaned close, turning his hand over to grip hers. His other palmed her face. It was the softest caress, like a whisper of air, but it made her blood thunder and hope stir.

'I underestimated you.'

Her jaw shot up. 'You did.' She'd bared her heart but she strove not to show how vulnerable she felt.

'The first time I saw you,' he murmured, 'I fell for you like a ton of bricks. Just watching you walk across that courtyard was like music and sunshine and the best vintage wine all rolled into one.'

Chiara's eyes widened. Fell for? Could it be…?

'That's right, *tesoro*. I fell for you that first day and I've been falling ever since.'

Chiara's heart gave an almighty thump as if it would burst free of her ribcage. The look in his indigo eyes mesmerised her.

'I wasn't taking any chances on you refusing to go out with me. I knew our brothers were in the same business. I've built hotels for Luca before, but I didn't see why that should come between us so I chose not to mention it. If you found out along the way, well' —his powerful shoulders lifted— 'that would be time enough.'

'Why didn't you just explain when I asked? I didn't believe you'd actually betrayed me when I came to see you, you know.' Hurt lingered at the memory of that night. 'I was sure it was a misunderstanding. All I needed was to hear you say it.'

'I'm sorry, Chiara, so sorry. I was a proud, thoughtless bastard. Of course I should have explained.' He breathed deep. 'You came in dressed like a million dollars, dripping with heirloom diamonds—'

'I was going to a ball!' What had her clothes to do with anything?

'And there I was, just in from a building site I'd been inspecting. Old boots, dust in my hair.'

Chiara sat back, amazement for a moment stealing her voice.

'Don't look at me like that!' His hold tightened. 'I know it was stupid. I know you don't care about that sort of thing. The fact my brothers and I grew up on a farm. That we had no money to start with.'

'Good!' she snapped, anger stirring.

'It didn't matter to you, but it did to me. I've always needed to prove myself and there was I, head over ears in love with a society princess and scared as hell. I've never been in love before either. I hadn't expected it. What man does?'

He loved her? Her heart danced, despite her shock.

Slow, glorious hope filled her.

Chiara remembered the bemused look in her brother's eyes when Jenna and he had their on-again off-again affair before they sorted themselves out. Did all men react to love like that, or just those who liked to be in total control? Could that really be what had happened to Gennaro? To think of them both struggling to hide their true feelings!

'Go on.'

Gennaro's expression changed. Sheepish was the word that came to mind. 'You say you were the coward?' He shook his head. 'I was petrified of what I felt. I hadn't planned to be tied down for years yet—'

'No one said anything about tying you down.' Though the idea of spending her life with Gennaro made her heart stall in delight.

'And in you came, accusing me of dishonesty. To a man who'd grown up with nothing but his family honour that was unforgivable.'

He raised his hand when she tried to speak.

'I know. I was unreasonable. You didn't actually accuse. But Luca was right. I was scared of what you made me feel so I lashed out rather than explain. I refused to justify myself on the grounds you should have trusted me from the first.' He shook his head. 'I don't pretend it was my finest moment.'

He gathered both her hands in his, holding them together almost as if in prayer, and something tugged at Chiara's heart.

'That was my big mistake. Foolishly I thought you should trust me, without all the facts, just because I said so. I used *honour* as some sort of test of your loyalty, as if I didn't know it would turn you away from me. What woman would put up with that? Of course you deserved a full explanation.'

Chiara stared up at Gennaro, reading the regret and pain on his face. They'd both been quick to judge. What a price they'd paid for that.

He lifted her hands, placing them on his chest. Beneath the warm cotton she felt his heart thundering. 'Like an idiot I thought you'd be back if you truly cared. I forgot you had your pride too.'

'And that I was hurt.'

A spasm tightened his face. 'And that I'd hurt you.' He shook his head. 'When I saw what I'd done, I tried to make amends. I called and left messages but you refused to have anything to do with me.'

To Chiara's surprise his eyes shone. 'I loved you all the more for standing up against me. Who'd have believed it?' His voice lowered as he leaned across the tiny table towards her. 'I was proud of the way you stood your ground, even while it sent me crazy, trying to find a way to reach you.'

'Really?' Chiara found she could smile. 'Remind me to do it again. I could—'

'Don't you dare! I'm not going through this again. You're mine.' His voice dropped to that low note that always sent a shiver of feminine delight through her. 'I'm never letting you go.'

'Perhaps I'll have something to say about that.' But in her heart, her glowing, full heart, she knew he was right. Neither of them were perfect. They'd have to work at building their relationship. But she loved him too much ever to walk away from him again. And if he loved her as much, well, the world looked suddenly brighter.

She looked around the tiny square of the small provincial town. For the first time she noticed the charm of the deep overhanging balconies, the ornate wood carvings, the window boxes bright with geraniums, the buildings across the road with quaint painted scenes on their walls.

'You're going to make me pay for my arrogance, aren't you?' He didn't sound at all perturbed.

Her lips twitched as she began to think of what form that payment might take. 'What makes you say that?'

'Just a feeling.' He lifted her hands and kissed them, one at a time. 'You do still love me?'

Humour fled at his expression. 'I still love you, Gennaro.'

'And I love you, Chiara.' He smiled and instantly she wondered what he was up to. He looked more than happy. He looked smug.

'What have you done?'

'Nothing.' But a grin split his face.

'Tell me, Gennaro, or I'll insist on driving your

car all the way to Milan.'

He winced, but a smile lurked at the corner of his mouth. 'There was a reason I brought you up to the Alto Adige.'

'Go on.'

He looked over her shoulder, his expression expectant. Chiara heard a car approach. Nothing else.

'I brought you here because this is my home town. Not this precisely.' He waved a hand towards the direction they'd come from. 'But the village at the bottom of the road to the resort.'

'The one we drove through on the way here?'

'Exactly. I didn't stop there because it doesn't have any boutiques. I knew you'd want fresh clothes for this morning.'

'Why?' Instinct told her there was more to this than she suspected.

Behind her a car slowed to a stop. Gennaro spared it one quick glance. 'Because I have one more surprise for you, my darling. I knew that as soon as I appeared in town with a gorgeous woman, word would reach my family. I've bought us an extra hour by coming here, further down the valley, but I knew the grapevine would work overtime from the moment we appeared in the town square.'

Both of them barefoot and looking disreputable.

Chiara frowned, her spine tingling in premonition. 'Who are you expecting, Gennaro?'

'Now, now, it's okay.' He kissed her hand, his lips lingering. When he looked up his smile had gone, replaced with a look so tender it stole her breath. 'I just want to convince you how much you mean to me.' He snagged a quick breath. 'What better proof of an Italian man's feelings than to have you meet his mother?'

Chiara stared. Her pulse kicked hard. 'Your mother?'

He chuckled, the sound like honey. 'Don't look so worried. She wants nothing more than for me to settle down with a lovely woman. Before you know it she'll be giving you tips on how to keep me under your thumb.'

'Is that really how mothers react to interloping women around here?' Tension twisted her stomach.

Gennaro cupped her cheek. 'Don't worry, *tesoro*. She's heard all about you. When Luca let slip what had happened between us she told me I was an idiot. She's a strong-minded woman herself and she's looking forward to welcoming the woman I love into the family.' Yet it wasn't the thought of his mother that held her attention. It was Gennaro. The way he looked at her made her feel… she couldn't put into words the happiness and hope blooming inside.

'None of that matters, Chiara. Nothing matters except that you're the woman I adore. Now and always. Will you be mine?'

Chiara took his hand in hers and lifted it to her mouth, pressing a kiss on the hard line of knuckle right where an old scar silvered his golden skin. 'You know I will. If you'll be mine. Now and always.'

BOUND TO THE
Italian Boss

Book 3, Hot Italian Nights

Thank you to Dr G, who braved marmots, mountains, snow and hairpin bends so I could collect inspiration for this story.

Chapter One

LUCA ACCELERATED OUT OF THE hairpin curve, feeling the sports car's big engine surge. The tarmac of the alpine pass streamed behind him as he headed south in a series of sweeping bends.

Ahead rose the familiar jagged-tooth mountains he knew from childhood.

His world had changed enormously from that rundown farmhouse in the high Italian Dolomite Mountains. His multinational hotel empire had taken hard work, long hours and a determination to accept nothing less than the best.

No wonder he'd had no time lately to indulge his love of speed.

Or for any other indulgence, he realised as the wind ruffled his hair, blowing away the last cobwebs from his meetings in Munich. His schedule had reached manic proportions. Even his long-suffering PA, the indomitable Allegra Davis, had begun to look strained.

Luca's mouth quirked. If the iron maiden started complaining, he really *was* pushing it.

Allegra lived for her career. She worked long hours no lover would tolerate and knew almost as much about the business as Luca. She'd been indispensable as he closed deals on the Thai resort and the Venetian palazzo and she ran his office like a well-oiled machine. Behind her unflappable calm lurked a dry humour he enjoyed almost as much as her impressive organisational skills.

They made a formidable team, anticipating each other in the way long term partners did. Or lovers.

Not that there was anything between him and Allegra. He never mixed work and sex. Nor did she, thankfully! He'd had enough trouble with starry-eyed temps. Besides, he preferred his women less…buttoned up.

Yet he'd found himself perversely enticed by her strait-laced demeanour and hints of an alluring feminine body beneath those boxy trouser suits.

Last week a pretty blonde in a barely-there dress had cemented herself to him at a business gala. Yet Luca hadn't been distracted by her, but by the memory of Allegra as he'd left the office half an hour before. For once her immaculate hair showed a hint of the long day they'd put in. Dark strands escaped to curl low, drawing attention to the barest hint of shadowed cleavage. He'd paused, inhaling the delicate scent of vanilla and female flesh as he reached for a file.

Even now, driving down the side of the mountain, he felt the frisson of awareness that had blindsided him that evening.

Allegra had worked for him a year and it was the first time he realised she had curly hair! With her tightly scraped buns he'd had no idea. Now, at the oddest times he found himself wondering how his no-nonsense PA would look with her hair loose. Was it shoulder-length? Longer? No. Any woman who wore those trendy but severe thick-rimmed glasses wasn't the sort to keep long, sexy hair.

He and Allegra had nothing in common except work.

His new year's resolution had been to kick back and occasionally take time to enjoy his success. To find time for skiing and mountaineering and, yes, speed.

The idea of his staid PA enjoying anything more dangerous than a ringside seat at his next corporate acquisition was laughable.

Luca slowed, shifting down as he approached another series of hairpin bends. Over the low-throated growl of the engine he heard the buzz of another motor. In the mirror he saw a flash of black hurtle down towards the curve he'd just rounded.

Luca grinned. Last time he'd ridden this pass he'd been in bike leathers, not business clothes. There was nothing like the rush of adrenalin with a big beast of an engine between your thighs as you swooped down, testing your nerve, skimming the outer edge of the road.

He slowed for a blind curve and a tourist bus chugged up in the other direction, barely making the turn. Then he was down to another hairpin bend, this time with clear vision beyond. As he touched the brakes the motorcycle closed behind him then cut the corner, swinging out then away down the straight. It was deftly done, with neat judgement both for the road and the bike's capabilities.

Luca was mentally applauding when he saw a blur of movement. A marmot ran right across the path of the bike. The rider braked, veered and just missed the animal. But the veer took the front wheel off the tarmac and onto the narrow gravel shoulder. The rear wheel followed.

There was a wobble, a skid and the bike began to right. Luca tapped his own brakes, willing the rider to succeed. But in that soft gravel it was almost impossible.

Seconds later, in what seemed slow motion, the bike and rider heeled over, sliding to a halt on the very edge of the sheer drop to the next curve of road.

Luca wrestled his own vehicle to an urgent stop just past the bike. He was out of the car in seconds, not bothering to reach for his phone. Reception here was patchy at best. He hoped for the rider's sake he didn't need an ambulance.

The acrid smell of rubber and gravel hit him, and sweet meadow grass where one tyre had dug a path on the extreme edge of the slope.

Luca hunkered beside the prone figure, heart hammering, adrenalin pumping. He couldn't see blood despite the tear in the leg of the rider's leathers. But the guy lay unmoving.

Dread rose. Had he hit his head?

'Where does it hurt?' He fought the instinct to reach out and investigate. Better to let the rider tell him, if he could.

'Everywhere.' The voice was soft and husky and somehow familiar. It must be a trick of imagination, fired by relief at discovering the rider was conscious.

'Can you move your legs?'

'Just give me a second.'

The second stretched out till finally the rider moved. First one arm then the other, slowly closing each hand. Then a ripple of motion—

'Don't sit up!'

Too late. The black clad figure rose on one elbow then lurched sideways. Luca grabbed one skinny upper arm, holding him steady. Was it a kid, rather than a man? That would explain the voice. And make his control of the bike even more remarkable. Only an experienced rider could have come so close to saving himself in the circumstances.

'I feel a bit woozy.'

'I'm not surprised. You bit the dirt with a lot of force.' His gaze strayed to the drop beside them and the next stretch of tarmac well below. Luca's belly lurched. If the rider had been less experienced, or less lucky, he'd be dead now.

But the guy had grit. Slowly, with only a hitch of breath betraying any pain, he sat higher, legs stretched out before him. Surely he couldn't have done that if he'd damaged his spine? As if in response to his silent thoughts the rider rotated first one foot then the other, then bent first one then the second knee.

Luca released a pent up breath. Years ago he'd been first on the scene when a novice had tried a black ski run and barely survived. The kid had never walked again.

'You're lucky to be alive.' The words burst out from the dam of half-buried memories.

'I know. I swear I saw my life flash before my eyes.' Again that strange sense of recognition as he heard that voice. But as it was muffled by the bike helmet that meant nothing.

'Let me help with the helmet.' Luca wouldn't be happy till he'd checked for injuries. The fact the rider was talking was excellent but——

'I can do it.'

Was it imagination or was the guy slow to move? If Luca didn't know better he'd say he read reluctance in the rider's movements, though logic told him it was more likely pain.

The black helmet rose and a froth of long, dark waves cascaded down past the rider's shoulders. Luca blinked, his brain scrambling to catch up with the evidence of his own eyes. The rider twisted away, putting the helmet on the ground, and the sun gleamed on an unexpected curve beneath the black biker's jacket. The curve of a female breast.

Slowly the woman turned her head. Eyes that were familiar yet unexpected met his. Unexpected because the woman he knew had plain brown eyes, not grey-blue the colour of the sky at dusk.

Yet the face was the same. Clear, pale skin, straight nose and a neat jaw. A familiar face, yet…different. Without thick-rimmed glasses there was nothing to distract him from those surprisingly lush lips. Or the stunning beauty of that bright gaze.

Luca frowned. Either he was going crazy or this woman was the almost-twin of his redoubtable PA. The woman he'd last seen in a charcoal trouser suit, high buttoned shirt and flat shoes. The woman whose idea of living dangerously was allowing one of the junior secretaries to order dinner when they worked late.

He blinked. It couldn't be. Allegra Davis was even now driving up from Milan to meet him at the alpine resort his brother Gennaro had just completed building. Unless she was already there, briskly beginning the site visit in anticipation of his arrival.

One thick leather glove rose and the woman pushed the hair back from her face. Hair that gleamed richly in the sunlight and smelled of vanilla.

'Hello, boss. Fancy meeting you here.'

Chapter Two

ALLEGRA'S LEG BURNED WHERE SHE'D hit the ground. But that was all. She'd been incredibly lucky. Right now any potential bruises seemed the least of her worries.

Hell! The look on his face…

She was as used to Luca's frowns as she was to his rare, blinding smiles that left her weak-kneed and reeling. That is, she was used to not showing her reaction to them. But this wasn't just any frown. This was something else – a scowl of disbelief and horror.

'Allegra?' His face paled. His deep voice sounded stretched.

He was in shock. And who could blame him?

The one thing he'd never expected to see, the one thing she'd guarded so carefully against revealing for the last twelve months, was the *real* Allegra Davis.

Her heart dipped as it had in the moments when she'd wrestled to keep the bike on track. When she'd been sure that in another second she'd be flying off the edge of the mountain to an early death.

Her eyes squeezed shut. This wasn't just an accident. It was disaster on a monumental scale.

'Allegra? Are you okay?' His deep, velvet over gravel voice plumbed new depths and suddenly he was around her, supporting her, his broad chest propping her back, his long legs stretched out on either side of hers, his arms gently enfolding her.

Allegra bit her bottom lip and commanded her stupid heart to stop that too-quick, too-unsteady rhythm. She was no fainting damsel in need of support. Even if her whole body quivered with the effects of shock and there was a burning throb down one leg.

She had a horrible suspicion that it wasn't the aftermath of the accident making her tremble so much as the reality of being in Luca De Laurentis's arms for the first and only time.

She swallowed hard, searching for her voice.

'I'm okay.'

As if that wisp of sound would convince any-one! She needed to do better. Especially when his response was to wrap himself more closely around her, as if afraid she was about to keel over.

When that animal had raced in front of her and the world had slowed to a series of freeze frame images, she'd turned ice cold. But now, safe against the blazing furnace of Luca's athletic frame, heat enveloped her. It numbed the ache in her leg and trickled into her bones, filling the empty places that she'd kept locked against any man. Or tried to. For months now she'd known she fought a losing battle, pretending all she felt for Luca was respect and admiration.

'You don't feel okay. You're shaking like a leaf.' The growl came from just behind her ear, stirring her hair, sending a shaft of longing right through her core. It felt so…intimate.

'I just came off a bike on the edge of a mountain.

What do you expect?' The words were supposed to come out clipped, even snarky. Instead she heard the tell-tale roughness and swallowed. She hoped he put it down to reaction to the fall. Surely he couldn't hear the longing she'd tried to suppress so long. Or the fear that suddenly, in one unguarded moment, she'd put at risk everything she'd worked for.

Luca's arms tightened, drawing her back till he took her weight. In thick motorcycle leathers she shouldn't be able to feel the dip and rise of his muscled chest, should she? It had to be imagination working overtime. But there was no mistaking the solid strength of the biceps encompassing her, or of those powerful thighs bracketing hers.

A tingling, burgeoning sensation began deep inside. An inexorable awakening of parts of her body Allegra usually had no reason to notice.

'What were you doing on that bike?'

She shrugged, but froze mid-movement as it emphasised the contact between their bodies. 'Same as you. Travelling to the new hotel.'

'From the north?'

That had been her mistake. She'd travelled up from Milan early, enjoying some long overdue downtime. She'd got to the empty hotel, still smelling of fresh timber and new-laid carpet, and found a place to park the bike out of sight. Luca wouldn't question how she'd travelled. Then, tomorrow, after he left for the city, she'd treat herself to another ride down through the mountains to the autostrada and Milan. Except once in the Dolomites, heady with joy from the freedom of the ride, she'd dumped her luggage and headed out for an extra hour's riding.

Stupid of her to be so self-indulgent. Her whole life was about control. Without that she'd never have landed the plum job she had now.

Control and deception.

Allegra shivered again. It wasn't deceit, precisely, to camouflage herself. Not when the alternative was no job or worse, being hit on and judged on her looks rather than her ability.

'I arrived early and thought I'd explore a little.'

'On a motorcycle?' Was that disapproval in his tone, or disbelief?

'If that was a question, then the answer is yes.' Allegra stirred, hard as it was to pull away from the comfort of that big body. 'It's not a crime to ride a bike, you know.'

Luca's arms tightened around her middle and part of her, the part that foolishly yearned for things that could never be, silently sighed.

'Not so fast.'

'Why, because you want to give me the third degree?' Anger whipped in her veins. What business was it of his to disapprove? 'What I do outside work is my business alone!'

Silence. The sort of silence where you'd hear a pin drop across a room. Or the easy working relationship they'd built crack right down the middle.

In the office they worked almost as partners and the key to that was mutual respect. Allegra had a sick feeling in her stomach that was about to change. She was overreacting. She knew it, but the guard she kept on her emotions when Luca was around had deserted her.

'I was going to say you shouldn't move too fast.

You don't yet know how badly you're injured.'

She turned her head and met his gleaming dark gaze.

Too close! So close she felt his breath warm on her face. She dragged in air through open lips and saw his gaze drop to her mouth.

Her pulse pounded hard and fast, faster than before, and at her back the rhythm of his heart quickened too.

That…thing was back again. The thing that more than once had made them both stop in their tracks in the middle of a totally ordinary day.

The sensation of something drawing them inexorably together, blocking out their surroundings and cocooning them in intimacy.

The thing that scared her witless.

'Then let me go and I'll be able to find out if I'm hurt.' She wriggled, pulling forward out of his hold, aware that she was only able to do so because he let her. Lying back against Luca De Laurentis confirmed in spades what she'd always suspected – that beneath the perfect Italian tailoring, his body was all hard-packed muscle.

She was stiff now the initial shock wore off, a little achy. But that was all so far.

Moments later she was kneeling and relieved to discover she seemed uninjured. Even the pain in her leg had receded to a dull ache, though she'd have a bruise there later. She shook her head. She'd been unbelievably lucky.

Reaction hit and Allegra shuddered. She longed for a hot bath and solitude. She didn't feel up to dealing with Luca now.

'How many fingers am I holding up?'

'Sorry?'

'You heard me.' His voice was crisp, totally businesslike. Allegra should be relieved. She shouldn't miss that gravelly edge she'd heard in his voice just minutes ago. Now he sounded more like the man she knew – controlled, ordered, and unemotional.

Automatically she turned. He was still too close, his dark, fathomless eyes fixing her to the spot. His tantalising spicy scent made her nostrils tingle and her stomach do a little shimmy of delight. His strong jaw had that determined set she knew meant he wasn't about to back down.

'Three fingers. I'm not concussed.' Allegra pushed her hair back from her face with a hand that shook. It was still there – that fine trembling. Maybe it was reaction to the accident after all. Her gaze travelled to the steep drop beside her and her stomach bottomed.

'Don't!'

Her head swung up and their gazes meshed. The impact of it shivered through her. 'Don't what?'

'Think about what might have happened.' His tone was terse, almost savage, and it struck her she'd never heard Luca quite so angry. Even the day his rival Raffaele Petri had beaten him to a once in a lifetime deal for a brilliant coastal resort. 'You're safe now. That's what matters.'

Allegra nodded.

Safe. He was right. That was the important thing.

But her cover was blown. Luca might not be peppering her with questions but she could tell by the searing intensity of his stare that he had plenty. About why she dressed the way she did, hid her real eye colour behind coloured contacts and shunned everything that might draw male attention.

'You're right, of course.' Slowly she got to her feet, pretending she didn't see his outstretched hand. The last thing she needed was to touch him. She felt too weak as it was.

Gingerly she stretched, relief rising as each bone and muscle worked as it should. There'd definitely be bruising, but somehow she'd escaped serious harm. Slowing for that hairpin bend had probably saved her life. She'd just been accelerating when—

'I told you not to think about it.' Suddenly he was before her, looming far too near. 'Come on.' His hand curled around the leather at her elbow.

'Where?'

'To the car. You're not up to riding down the mountain, even if the bike's okay, which I doubt.'

It was on the tip of Allegra's tongue to argue but she wasn't stupid. She was so shaken up she wouldn't trust herself on a pushbike right now, much less the powerful motorcycle.

Silently she nodded and let him lead her to the low-slung sports car, a prestige symbol of fluid power in cobalt blue.

'What?' One sleek, dark eyebrow rose as he opened the door. Trust Luca to read her expression even when she hadn't spoken.

'Just wondering why a man who drives a car like this should disapprove of motorbikes.'

He pushed her gently into the soft bucket seat and stepped back, towering before her like some thunder god with that scowl marring his handsome face. To her chagrin, anger only emphasised the charisma of those strong, compelling features.

'I don't disapprove of them. I'm a bike rider

myself.'

'So it's just the idea of *me* riding one that you don't like?' Why she pushed it, Allegra didn't know. Except there was an excess of adrenalin still pumping in her bloodstream and she needed an outlet for this sudden surge of emotion. Under normal circumstances she was the one to pour oil on troubled waters, not pick a fight.

Or maybe her anger was fuelled by disappointment. For the first time Luca had glimpsed the real her, not the sedate, buttoned up version she'd learnt to adopt for corporate survival. It hurt that instead of…liking what he saw, he so obviously disapproved.

The fall must have addled her brain. She didn't want his approval, or for him to be interested in her personal life. That's why she'd adopted camouflage in the office, to avoid intimacy.

Yet somehow that strategy had backfired. These last months the idea of intimacy with her employer wasn't quite as taboo as it had once been.

Slowly Luca folded his arms over his chest and Allegra had to call on all her control not to follow the movement, but keep her eyes on his. With his shirt sleeves rolled up to reveal strong, sinewy forearms, his eyes narrowed and glossy, dark hair rumpled, he looked like some mountain marauder, not a captain of industry.

'I don't like the idea of you in danger. It was bad enough watching the bike skid off the road. When I realised it was you…' He shook his head, his jaw setting like stone. And all of a sudden it wasn't indignation Allegra felt but a strange, fluttery excitement as if her heart beat too high in her chest.

'I'm fine. Like you said – just don't think about it.'

'Do as I say, not as I do?' His mouth kicked up at the corner and her pulse with it.

Any more of this and she'd need medical attention for her heartrate. Because his half smile was so rare and devastating it did ridiculous things to her, no matter how well she hid behind her mask of professional indifference.

'Sit and rest while I check the bike.'

Allegra opened her mouth to say she was perfectly capable of checking the bike herself then snapped it shut. Her legs were like jelly and it was heaven just sitting.

Fascinated, she watched as Luca righted the bike, then proceeded to pore over it with deft efficiency.

'A few scrapes but it seems sound.' He started it, listening intently to the throb of the motor, before shutting the engine. 'When we have phone coverage I'll organise for it to be collected and checked out. It shouldn't take long.'

And leave her precious bike abandoned on the roadside?

She didn't say it aloud but he must have read her thoughts. Luca sometimes had that uncanny knack.

'I could ride it down myself but I doubt you feel up to driving just yet.'

Allegra stared at the car's dashboard. Any other day and she'd jump at the chance to control such a precision-engineered vehicle. But not now when her legs felt like wet noodles and her hands trembled. She slid her hands under her thighs, not wanting Luca to notice. He'd just fuss.

'I'll move it along behind the rock wall back there till the mechanic arrives.'

Numbly she watched him move the bike. Then he returned to the car and without pausing, bent and scooped her legs up into the well of the car, gently closing the door.

Allegra was wondering how she still felt the imprint of his hand on her leg when he got in the driver's seat, filling all available space with his big body and his electric presence. Once more those hard hands reached for her, this time drawing the seatbelt across her body and clipping it into place quickly and efficiently as if he hadn't felt the brush of his knuckles across her breasts.

Allegra's nipples budded against her T shirt and she shut her eyes, profoundly grateful for the thick leather jacket that must hide that deeply feminine and wholly unstoppable response.

The engine throbbed into life and she felt the car swing gently onto the road.

'So, Allegra.' That soft-as-silk voice slid through her like a caress, making her eyes pop open warily. 'Are you going to explain the masquerade?'

Chapter Three

WIDE, DARK-FRINGED EYES MET HIS and something punched deep into his gut. Anger, confusion, and hurt that the one woman he'd trusted above all others had perpetrated such a fraud on him. His belly clenched in denial.

Those eyes he thought he knew so well stared back, bright, unfamiliar, more beautiful than he'd ever imagined.

The woman he thought he'd known had made a fool of him every day when she'd hidden herself behind camouflage that had turned flagrant beauty into bland, understated primness.

Though he'd sensed the beauty in her, hadn't he? She'd intruded far too much on his thoughts.

He'd grown…fond of her. And all the time she'd been secretly laughing at him.

'Do you even *need* glasses?' The words shot out, abrupt and bitter.

She blinked and her pupils dilated, making the blue-grey look almost silver. So clear and pure. So deceptive!

Luca set his teeth and focused on the long smooth ribbon of road, then the next tight curve. He manoeuvred the car on auto pilot, his attention on the woman sitting so stiffly beside him.

'Sometimes. For reading.' Her voice was muffled,

a shadow of her usual crisp tones. The aftermath of shock? Or from being found out?

Impatience ground through him. 'Yet you wear them all the time in the office.'

Silence.

'You owe me an explanation.'

'Let's wait till we get off the mountain. I'd rather you concentrated on the road.'

Of course she did. It was in her interests to delay. But Luca had no compunction about pressing the issue. Years of commercial experience had taught him to capitalise on weakness. He wasn't giving Allegra time to stitch together any excuses.

'I can drive and listen. Tell me now.'

He paused and waited for a response that didn't come and his anger turned icy. No man appreciated being made a fool of. Especially by the woman he—

'Tell me now, or when we get to the hotel site I'll accept your resignation.' She'd lied to him too long.

Allegra's breath hissed in and he fought the impulse to retract the words. Yes, she was off-centre, probably hurting and in shock, but he needed to *know*.

He couldn't afford to be distracted by sympathy. Bad enough he'd had to battle to let her go earlier. It had been far too hard to unlock his arms and let her pull away from him.

The realisation it was Allegra on that out of control bike… Luca couldn't recall being so terrified in all his life.

From the corner of his eye he saw her slender fingers knot over black leather trousers, her discarded gloves on her thigh. Guilt swamped him as instantly his mind conjured an image of her kneeling before him on the roadside, black leather stretched taut over the ripe swell of a perfect, female backside. He'd discovered more about her body in the last ten minutes than in twelve months working together.

'Is it industrial espionage? Are you working for Raffa Petri? Or for Fabrizio Armati?' That was more likely. Armati had an axe to grind since Luca had beaten him to the Venetian palazzo that, when renovated, would make a superb luxury hotel.

Armati had even accused him, Luca, of having a spy in his office, feeding him information on the deal! But Luca's success was due to sheer hard work and a huge dollop of luck. He'd been in Venice at just the right time. A chance conversation at a party had led him to the elderly aristocrat needing to sell his ancient palazzo.

'I'm not working for anyone but you.' Allegra's voice was flat. It annoyed him that he couldn't read it. 'If I was going to betray you I've had plenty of opportunities. But you know I haven't.'

It was true. In fact the Venetian deal had succeeded, in part, because of her. The vendor had taken a liking to Allegra with her restrained courtesy, her sober clothes and that surprising dry sense of humour. The fact that, despite being born and raised in England, Allegra's Italian was coloured by a touch of her mother's Venetian dialect might have helped too.

'What else have you lied about?' He frowned as he shifted down for another bend, then another. It couldn't be her references. They'd been checked meticulously before he'd even interviewed her.

'Nothing!'

She sounded outraged, as if butter wouldn't melt in her mouth. As if *he* was the one in the wrong and she the innocent!

Luca slanted her a sideways look and saw her in profile, her bottom lip caught in her teeth as if biting back emotion.

Ridiculously guilt sliced through him.

'Then why? Why the charade? If it's some joke at my expense—'

'It's not! It's got nothing to do with you.' Gleaming eyes met with his and something unravelled in his chest. He turned back to the road.

'Yet I'm the one you lied to for the past year.'

'I'm sorry.' Her voice was small but clear. 'I thought it was necessary and then later…well, it was too late.'

'Explain.' Luca hauled the car around the last of the hairpin bends and accelerated. Not too far to go. Impatience filled him. He wanted answers, *now*.

'I'm good at my work, you know that. I'm diligent and productive. I work long hours and I manage pressure well.'

Luca said nothing. If she was after a reference she was barking up the wrong tree.

'Don't stop now, *cara*. I'm all ears.'

Allegra cringed at the sarcasm in that pseudo endearment. She'd never been his dear and never would be.

It was some vast cosmic joke that she'd gone to such lengths to put a wall between herself and the men she worked with, negating any chance that they'd see her as desirable, only to find herself falling for her boss.

She, who'd vowed that work and personal life would stay strictly separate.

As if she had a personal life these days!

She turned and viewed his taut profile. Even the short beard he'd grown in the past couple of weeks couldn't disguise the stark clamp of his jaw. The tendons in his neck stood proud and his nostrils flared.

He was absolutely furious and keeping it in by the smallest of margins.

Fine. He wanted the truth. He could have it.

Allegra knotted her hands in her lap and faced forward, watching as they approached a stand of dark trees and the road flattened into a high valley.

'I've always worked hard, given a hundred per cent of myself to my work. But I discovered early that some people expect more.' She paused, swallowing. 'Far more than anyone should have to give.'

There was a long silence.

'Are you talking about sex?' She couldn't read his tone but the steel in it made the fine hairs on her arms prickle and rise.

'Yes.' She tipped her chin higher. *She* had nothing to be ashamed of. 'I was sexually harassed.' Allegra was proud of her cool tone, like water slipping over grimy stones. If only the memories could be so easily washed away.

'You didn't complain to your boss?'

A snort of derision escaped. 'Who do you think was doing the…harassing?' She swallowed, tasting bitterness on her palate. Harassing sounded clinical and simple. So much easier than *groping* or *attempted rape*. Just as well her big brother had taught her how to defend herself. Sam Parkinson had ended up with severe bruising and a damaged ego and Allegra had escaped unharmed, if you didn't count losing her job. And then there was the sick, panicky feeling in her stomach whenever a man got too close.

Though that had worn off, hadn't it? She and Luca regularly worked late, closeted in his office, and he'd never in all that time made her feel uncomfortable. On the contrary, she'd found herself spinning *what if* fantasies about him.

'Allegra?' His voice was sharp. 'I asked if you were hurt.'

'No.' Not in ways that showed. 'But I was angry. He was the one in the wrong but because he was the manager I was the one who had to leave a good job.'

'You didn't take him to court?'

Allegra shook her head. 'And go through every incident again in public?'

'It happened more than once?'

His tone made her turn to find his anger hadn't subsided. Not if the white-knuckled grip on the steering wheel was an indicator.

'There was a build up.' She'd kept telling herself she could handle it, but of course that was impossible. 'And he wasn't the only one.' She hesitated, then heard the words spill out. 'I found out later there was an informal bet on among some of the men, to see who could get me to…' Her throat closed and to her horror she found herself blinking.

It must be the aftermath of the accident, making her feel wobbly. The rest was history. Her year in Italy, working with Luca, had shoved it all well and truly into a past that seemed like a bad dream now.

'Bastards. You should have pressed charges.'

Allegra shrugged. 'Yes. I know that now. There was an internal enquiry though and several staff lost jobs. The CEO offered to give me a promotion, working for him, but I just wanted to get away.'

'Which is when you came to Italy.'

She nodded. 'It was a new start.'

'Yet you didn't trust me? You felt you had to hide your real self? Why? Because you thought I might attack you?'

Chapter Four

LUCA WAS TORN BETWEEN SYMPATHY and outrage. Something caught in his chest at the idea of Allegra at the mercy of a man who wouldn't take no for an answer. A man who used his position of authority to coerce. Of a group of men betting on getting her into bed.

His mouth curled with distaste at the scenario.

But to believe he, *Luca,* was the same? To go to such lengths to camouflage herself… It was a vicious blow to his honour.

'If you thought I was going to jump you, why take the job?'

From the corner of his eye he saw her flinch and instantly regretted his harsh tone. But he needed to know. Surely he'd never done anything that could be misconstrued? He might be demanding, but he'd always treated her with respect.

'I took the job because you're the best and I knew I was beyond lucky to have a chance to work with you.'

The tight feeling in his chest eased a little. But at the core was a tension he suspected wouldn't disappear until he found out who'd tormented her. And made them pay. Knowing Allegra had been preyed upon like that aroused a surge of implacable hostility against those responsible, a need for retribution.

He swung up the road to the newly-completed ski lodge and parked the car in the gravel forecourt. But he barely took in the unique building with its soaring roof, huge windows and daring design.

He switched off the engine and twisted in his seat, his absolute focus on Allegra. It was an odd sensation, seeing the woman he knew so well who somehow was an entirely different person.

The neat, obstinate angle of the jaw was the same, the straight nose and the slender throat. But the blue-grey flash of her eyes was arrestingly different, and her mouth looked more lush and ripe without those serious glasses as a counterpoint.

As for her hair… Luca's fingers twitched at the idea of running his hand through those lush sable ripples.

Guilt hit with the force of a mountain avalanche. She'd just been in an accident. She was clearly distressed at revealing the abuse she'd suffered and here he was, imagining an altogether more intimate connection between them.

'So why the costume? I assume the glasses aren't needed?'

She pursed her mouth but instead of the action flattening her lips, it made them pout in a way he found far too delectable. Luca raked a hand through his hair, searching for the equilibrium he'd lost the moment he saw the crash. No, the moment Allegra had lifted the helmet and met his stare with that diamond-bright gaze.

'No, they're clear glass. They're—'

'A prop. But why did you think it necessary?'

Luca was proud of being a fair employer, even if he demanded the absolute best of his staff. Any hint of sexual harassment would be crushed mercilessly in his company.

She lifted her shoulders jerkily. 'I didn't know if it was necessary. I didn't think so but it seemed a reasonable precaution.' Her gaze flickered. 'Better safe than sorry. I seem to attract the wrong sort of attention.'

'You're beautiful.' The words were out before he'd considered them, but it was true. There was a gentle yet utterly sensuous beauty about Allegra that even her drab disguise couldn't conceal.

He watched her eyes dilate at his words. Her lips parted and again he felt that tug of awareness, deep within.

'But that's no excuse for them molesting you.' Pressure built inside at the thought and Luca had to make a conscious effort to draw down his shoulders and unclench his fists. His voice scratched his throat. 'I can't believe you thought I was like that. Or that you'd work for me in that case.'

'I didn't.' She moved, one hand lifting towards him before dropping back. 'But I couldn't be *sure*.' Her lips twisted. 'You have to admit you've got a reputation as a ladies man. And you have trouble keeping executive PAs. It made me wonder.'

Luca laughed, but the sound was mirthless. 'I had the same PA for years until she decided she wanted more time with her grandchildren. Since then I've had trouble keeping one because I seem to have a target painted on my back. Rich, single, possible meal ticket.'

'And hunky.' Her eyes widened and she froze.

She looked as surprised as he was. Luca stilled. Heat coiled tight and hard in his belly at the idea of her attracted to him. The Allegra Davis he knew would never describe her employer as hunky.

But this was a new Allegra, wasn't it? Or more correctly, an Allegra she'd never revealed before.

Faint colour washed her cheeks and he decided to ignore the comment. 'I found they were more interested in trying to seduce me than in doing a decent job. You have no idea what a godsend you were. Capable, efficient, every bit as exceptional as your references said.'

'Were?' Was that fear in her eyes?

What, did she think he'd sack her for her masquerade?

But then, he'd threatened to do just that if she didn't come clean, hadn't he?

'Are,' he affirmed. 'You're the best assistant I've ever had.'

The colour was back in her too pale face but this time her eyes glowed too, and there was a hint of a smile at the edges of those ripe lips.

'Thank you.' She paused, her expression growing serious. 'So that means I still have a job?'

Luca's ego was bruised because she'd thought she needed to go to such lengths to protect herself. But logically he understood her thinking.

'Of course. We make a good team.' He nodded to the empty building before them. 'And there's a lot of work waiting for us. I'm relying on you.'

Chapter Five

*H*E WAS RELYING ON HER.

Allegra didn't know whether to be pleased or nervous.

Pleased. Of course she was. The last thing she wanted was to lose the job she adored, working for the man she—

Ruthlessly she scraped her hair back, deftly tugging it high and twisting it into a neat coil on the back of her head. Long practice meant not a strand escaped. That was better. Now she felt, and looked, like the Allegra Davis who could handle anything her demanding boss threw at her.

Except he wasn't just a demanding boss. He was a caring one too.

Luca must have called the nearest medical practice before they even left the scene of her spill. They'd only been here at the hotel ten minutes when a doctor had arrived to give her a thorough check up. Allegra had no option but to submit to an examination, and secretly she'd been relieved when the doctor confirmed her own assessment of no significant injuries. She'd been very lucky.

Now, after a hot shower and a strong coffee, she felt ready to face Luca.

She smoothed her hands down the navy trouser suit with its deliberately concealing cut.

She remembered the lightweight skirts and jackets she'd worn when she worked in London. There'd been bright colours and the occasional pattern, in keeping with the woman she'd been then. Nothing revealing, nothing provocative, but clothes that were sunnier, more like the real her.

For a second resentment rose, that she'd felt it necessary to dress, not for herself, but to hide her figure. But after a year, she'd grown accustomed to the boxy suits, even found a strange liberation in hiding behind them, as if by playing down her femininity she was free to excel professionally.

How would Luca react if she came to work in a tangerine jersey skirt and cute black cropped jacket?

Allegra snorted. It wasn't going to happen. She'd left that outfit behind in the UK. Anyway, she wasn't dressing for Luca but herself. She was *comfortable* in this. Really!

It was strange though, how she felt bare without her clear glasses. She'd grown used to wearing them. There was no point putting them on, or her coloured contacts, now Luca had seen her without them.

So the woman looking back at her in the mirror of the partially completed resort bedroom looked disturbingly unfamiliar. A woman who wasn't the same as the one who'd been victimised in London. Nor was she the one who'd risen to every challenge Luca had set.

Nervous tension danced down her spine. Strain was natural, facing Luca after deceiving him so long. He'd taken everything incredibly well once the shock had worn off and she'd explained her reasons. In fact, his anger over what had happened in her previous job had been palpable and comforting.

Now she knew Luca, she realised her early caution with him, and her camouflage, had been unnecessary. He wasn't the sort to take advantage of an employee. He didn't have that selfish, bullying style and he kept his sex life well away from the office.

The man was driven, proud and focused on success.

And charismatic, generous and mind-numbingly sexy.

Allegra shook her head, her mouth thinning. She couldn't afford to think of him that way.

She turned, slipped her feet into sensible, low-heeled shoes and grabbed her electronic tablet.

It was time to show Luca she was as professional and efficient as ever. Even if she moved a little more gingerly after her fall.

But when she walked into the lobby, Luca too had undergone a transformation. Gone were the business clothes she was accustomed to. Instead he wore faded jeans that clung to powerful thighs and a shirt with sleeves rolled up, leaving bare his darkly tanned forearms and a V of bronzed flesh at the collar.

Allegra swallowed, her throat suddenly lined with sandpaper.

He turned when the project manager he was talking with pointed to the deep balcony across the front of the main building. Her gaze dropped from wide shoulders to those jeans, filled out to perfection from behind as well as from the front.

A pulse of something hard and urgent throbbed through her.

Luca De Laurentis was extravagantly appealing in his dark suits and crisp shirts, but in casual gear he made her heart hammer so loud it was a wonder he hadn't heard and turned around. Instead he was engrossed in a discussion about outdoor furniture and the question of summer shade for the guests using the hotel outside the ski season.

Allegra pressed a hand to her racing heart and told herself to get a grip. So she was attracted to the man. She'd been able to hide that in the office by focusing on work. She'd do the same here. Simple.

If only he didn't look altogether too enticing in casual gear.

The project manager's phone rang and he excused himself, moving away to take the call. Luca pivoted on his heel, his gaze locking with hers instantly, as if he knew unerringly where she was.

Heat washed her throat and to her horror her breasts swelled against her black lace demi-cup bra.

Surely she imagined the sizzle flaring between them? Luca hadn't moved, his expression hadn't changed. He just stood, *looking* at her, and fierce heat exploded in her belly.

Allegra lifted her hand to her head to adjust her glasses, then remembered she wasn't wearing them. The realisation made her unaccountably nervous. As if she needed a shield! Luca was her boss. He wasn't interested in her as anything but the woman who kept his business running smoothly.

Yet that silent stare unnerved her. Her tongue slicked out to moisten dry lips and his gaze dropped to her mouth. Lace scratched her burgeoning nipples and liquid heat pooled deep at her centre. She blinked, thrown completely by the depth of her response. It was one thing to have him feature in her most erotic dreams. She was a young, healthy woman, after all. But this blatantly sexual response, especially when she was supposed to be working, was scary new territory.

Allegra was still reeling when he smiled and approached. His smile was easy, like the ones he usually bestowed, and suddenly the febrile tension eased, as if he'd flicked off a switch.

'Are you sure you're up to this? If you need to rest today—'

'No, I'm okay. Though I'm glad there's already hot water here. That shower and the painkillers got rid of any stiffness.' She still felt a little churned up but the remedy for that, surely, was to focus on work rather than think about those slow-motion moments of horror on the mountain road.

He surveyed her silently for what seemed an age before he nodded. 'Okay, let's start. There's a lot to get through.' One dark eyebrow arched mischievously. 'Though you didn't need to wear a suit for a site inspection.'

She shrugged, willing herself not to stare at the picture of physical male perfection before her. Instead she met his dark eyes. 'It's what I wear for work.'

'I like you without the glasses,' he murmured unexpectedly and suddenly there it was again, that thread of heat curling through her insides. Then, to her surprise he tilted his head and grinned. 'Though I confess I rather liked them too.'

Liked her heavy glasses? Was he mad?

'You don't believe me?'

'I'm just surprised.'

'They made you look like a very prim librarian.' There was a gleam in his eye that made her wonder for one foolish moment if he had a secret fantasy about prim librarians. Until he nodded to her tablet, suddenly all business.

'Let's start in the kitchens. There's been a glitch with some of the commercial equipment. You may need to assist the project manager in following that up. Get someone from the office to chase it.'

He turned and led the way towards the back of the building.

It was a relief to be back on solid ground again, where Luca treated her solely as his indispensable PA.

Wasn't it?

'Right. I'll have someone get onto the replacement ovens straightaway. Now, about scheduling the launch promotion…'

Luca watched his PA rattle off the daunting 'to-do' list they'd spent the afternoon compiling. She spoke with her usual quick precision and an excellent grasp of the priorities. There was even a smile as she conferred with his project manager. She looked like she enjoyed the challenge of so much work to get the resort ready.

No doubt about it, Allegra Davis *was* the most efficient, capable employee in his company. Even if he'd spent all afternoon distracted by the unfamiliar flash of those remarkable eyes, and the lush fullness of her mouth. Every time she spoke, and particularly when she said his name, it was an effort to drag his attention from those too-kissable lips.

Luca dragged a hand round the back of his neck, trying to ease the strain of tight muscles. This was his right hand woman, the one he'd worked with closely for twelve months. He couldn't afford to see her as anything other than his super-organised assistant. Even if she'd morphed in one day from the woman he respected and liked, to one he respected, liked and wanted to undress.

He shoved his hands in his jeans pockets and turned to the window, leaving the others to their discussion.

It wasn't just the revelation of how beautiful Allegra was. Though that had hit him like a ton of bricks when she'd turned to him, her hair streaming around her shoulders, her bright eyes wide.

It was the discovery that there was far more to the woman who'd already attracted him even in her sombre, unflattering suits and too-serious glasses. Today he'd discovered a side to Allegra that spoke to something vital inside him. Far from being buttoned-up and sedate, she loved to ride, loved the power and thrill of biking on the magnificent, dangerous roads he adored. There was a vibrancy, and a vulnerability about her that drew him.

Luca set his jaw. That was another reason he couldn't act on this attraction. It was one thing to fantasise in the dead of night about stripping the glasses and suit from his PA to discover the flesh and blood woman beneath. But anything more was impossible when she'd been the victim of sexual harassment. Actual sexual assault, if his hunch was correct. That would explain the lengths she'd gone to hide herself.

He couldn't, absolutely wouldn't, make a move on a woman who'd been victimised like that, especially by a previous boss.

'Luca?' Her soft voice made him spin round. 'Is everything okay?'

She was right beside him, frowning up and he caught that light fragrance of vanilla and warm, feminine flesh. He swallowed, telling himself that once today was over and they were back in the office he'd manage to treat her as he always had.

'No.' He looked down into her beautiful face and knew things were far from okay. The attraction he'd felt for so long had blossomed today into something so urgent and powerful, it could undermine not only their working relationship but the clockwork precision of his world. 'I want to check on a few things outside before we finish up.'

He glanced down at her slim-fitting, leather shoes. They were low-heeled and sensible. But the resort nestled on a steep slope and the landscaping hadn't been completed. 'You'd better stay here and make a start on those calls.'

She nodded. Was it imagination or was that a shadow of disappointment across her features?

'Is there any news of my bike?'

'Sorry. I forgot to mention that. A mechanic I know has had a look at it and reckons it's in pretty good shape. He's giving it a once over and will deliver it,' he shot a look at his watch, 'soon.'

'A mechanic you *know*?' Her head tilted to one side as she watched him quizzically.

'I come from here.' He waved to the panorama

of jagged-toothed, snow-topped mountains that eased down into high alpine valleys of green. 'I grew up further down this very valley.'

Much as he'd loved the place he hadn't been able to get out quickly enough. Career options in the mountains were limited and he'd craved the excitement of city living and the challenge of building his own corporate enterprise.

'You were so lucky! I'm imagining lots of skiing, not to mention riding those fabulous alpine passes.' Allegra's eyes shone as she took in the vista.

'You like skiing?' He didn't know why he was surprised. He'd already learned his buttoned-up assistant wasn't the staid woman he'd imagined.

She nodded. 'I like the thrill of it.' Those luscious lips twisted. 'Anything with speed has always appealed. Even go-kart racing.' She turned back to him, a rare, unguarded smile lighting her face, and he felt the impact like a whack to the solar plexus. 'What a fabulous place to grow up. I lived in London and there was no ski slope on the doorstep.'

Luca shrugged, tamping down his fascination at this glimpse of a woman who shared his own passions. Or maybe it was a fascination with that alluring mouth.

'You're right. I was lucky. But on the downside there were the hours chopping wood to keep the old house warm through the long winter. And there was no money for a motorbike. The first time I rode this pass it was on a pushbike and my thighs ached for days after.'

It had been worth it though, for the mad thrill of speeding down the other side, so fast he knew he diced with death. But he'd survived and gone on to other thrills, most recently in the corporate sector.

'So you're visiting your family?' Allegra gestured to the first of the small towns just visible at the far end of the valley.

'Tomorrow. Tonight I stay here as we planned.' Because he wanted to experience the place, even in its unfinished state. An overnight stay would consolidate his ideas. It would also give him time to notice any final details they'd missed. He was a perfectionist when it came to his resorts and this one, a collaboration with his brother Gennaro, and built in his own home territory, was particularly special.

The only problem was, he realised as Allegra nodded and turned away, that the pair of them would be here alone. His project manager was going home to his heavily pregnant wife. There'd be no-one else in the almost-finished resort but Allegra.

Once that wouldn't have been a problem. But now...

The woman who was completely off limits grew more tempting by the moment.

Chapter Six

ALLEGRA SIPPED HER WINE AND tried for the hundredth time tonight not to stare. The trouble was, Luca was eminently worth staring at.

Her eyes fixed on the play of firelight across the hard, intriguing planes of his face as he leaned towards the vast stone fireplace and added a log to the fire that took the chill off the night air.

The darkness beyond the circle of fire and lamplight was a constant reminder they were alone in the building. Tomorrow it would be busy with decorators and other staff but tonight it was just the pair of them.

A delicate thrill of awareness, of unexplored possibilities, feathered her spine.

It scared her into speech.

'I like your brother's wine.' She lifted her glass in salute, surprised at how little remained.

'I'm glad. Aurelio is a talented wine maker and his product is in demand. I'm lucky he's agreed to supply the restaurant here.' Luca picked up the bottle and topped up her glass.

Strange that they'd got to the end of the bottle and she hadn't noticed. She didn't drink much and never around Luca, preferring to keep alert. But tonight, replete from the delicious food that had been provided for them, tired from the long day and the adrenalin spike of her accident, Allegra felt her guard dropping.

Luca sank into the chair beside her and stretched out his long legs in a lazy sprawl. Her mouth dried as she took in the powerful muscles straining the ancient denim of his jeans.

His tailored suits were perfect for his straight-shouldered, slim-hipped frame, but they concealed rather than revealed. Now, so close she could smell the warm, spice scent of his skin, mingled with sweet wood smoke, Allegra was more intensely aware of him than she'd ever been in the office. Preternatural sensitivity made her whole body hum.

Restlessly she shifted, taking another sip of delicious wine.

They'd begun the evening on opposite sides of the fireplace, on two chairs Luca had brought from their bedrooms since the luxurious leather lounges designed for this vast lounge room hadn't yet arrived.

Through dinner they'd talked, not of work, but subjects they'd never discussed before. About him learning to ski as soon as he could walk. About bike riding, kayaking and hang-gliding. It was as if today had peeled away the professional layers so they felt comfortable revealing more personal interests. They had so much in common it was like speed dating and finding the perfect man.

Her heart thudded.

Luca wasn't the perfect man. But tonight it was hard to remember he was her employer.

They'd begun sharing photos from their phones. Him of white water rafting in Colorado and she of a ski trip to Austria. Somewhere during the evening Luca had moved the chairs together to make the sharing easier. But now Allegra was hypersensitive to the fact she only had to move a fraction and their elbows would touch.

She shivered. The knowledge they were alone in this place added an altogether new dimension to their easy camaraderie. A piquancy of danger, for beneath the chat and the air of relaxation rippled an undercurrent of attraction.

Always in the past she'd been able to ignore it and bury herself in work. To tell herself the attraction was one-sided and thrust it behind the thick buttress of her reserve. To pretend it didn't exist.

But tonight… tonight it was impossible to ignore.

Besides, she'd always found it hard to resist the thrill of danger.

'Allegra, are you all right?' The husky timbre of Luca's voice caught at something in her chest and lower, deep down inside.

She turned to find his dark eyes locked on her.

The ripple became a shiver of longing. Of anticipation.

For the expression in Luca's eyes wasn't business-like or even bland. It seared through her with an intensity that turned her bones soft. Heat sparked and shimmered across her skin, and drove hard right to the core of her.

It was the look of a man who saw, not a work colleague, but a woman he wanted.

No, the woman he craved.

Allegra blinked, telling herself she was embroidering. Luca didn't *crave* her.

And even if he did… She waited for the sliver of

unease to pierce her. For the tawdry reality check of realising her boss was hitting on her.

But it wasn't like that.

This felt a million miles from what had happened in London.

Luca didn't make a move. All he did was watch her with those fathomless eyes, his jaw clenched while a pulse ticked hard at the base of his throat. Crazily, she wanted to lean over and lick the spot. Feel the thrum of his blood against her tongue and taste his skin.

A shiver ripped through her from scalp to toe, drawing her skin tight and pulling her nipples into needy points. She felt the scrape of them against her bra with every shortened breath.

Did Luca know? Could he sense the arousal swamping her body?

Common sense told her she needed to leave, make her excuses and head for her room. Remaining here, in this suddenly charged atmosphere, was incredibly reckless. And experience had taught her the hard way to be cautious.

Then Luca's mouth flattened and his nostrils flared as if he was drawing in her scent.

It felt incredibly intimate.

From the corner of her vision Allegra realised his hands had clenched into fists on his thighs, but he didn't reach for her.

No, there was nothing tawdry about this. This wasn't like being trapped next to the photocopier, Sam Parkinson's whisky breath after his long lunch sour in her nostrils. She stiffened as she recalled soft fingers groping the buttons on her blouse as Parkinson tried to block her escape with his fleshy frame.

'What are you thinking?' Luca's words were so soft they were a caress. She imagined she felt them, tiny puffs of air, feathering her cheek and mouth. Her lips tingled and her already dry mouth turned arid with desire.

She swallowed hard and tried to stuff all the feelings she'd let loose back into the box where she usually kept them.

Except Luca wouldn't let her look away. He didn't touch her, didn't coerce her, but there was no way Allegra could turn her head and sever the connection sizzling in the air between them.

'Allegra?'

'I'm thinking about my old boss, in London.' The words spilled out before she'd considered them and instantly Luca's head snapped back. His eyes turned blank. His features pared down as she watched, cheeks hollowing and jaw jutting.

'I'd never hurt you, Allegra. You must know that. You're safe with me.' He swung his head around to stare at the fire and immediately she sagged in her seat. It was as if the current of energy running between them had been snapped off. She felt trembly and weak, and sure in the knowledge Luca wouldn't touch her unless she wanted it. Yet that didn't make her feel safe precisely. More like…

Bereft. That was the word. She felt bereft.

'It's getting late.' His deep voice sounded as tight as the clamp of her ribs around her overfull heart. 'I'm going to turn in.'

He moved, ready to lever himself up from the chair but froze when Allegra put her hand on his.

His was much larger and broader than hers.

And hard and hot. She swallowed, suddenly over-whelmed by his sheer masculinity.

Luca stilled. She'd swear he wasn't even breathing.

She, on the other hand, was breathing too fast. Did he hear?

'Maybe I don't want to be safe.'

He twisted around, his forehead knotted into a frown.

'You're tired.' Yet he made no move to shift again, or to remove her hand.

'I'm not tired, Luca.' Even saying his name felt different tonight. *Tasted* different.

She circled her dry mouth with her tongue and his gaze dropped to her mouth. Instantly her lips tingled. Did they pout of their own accord? Surely she hadn't planned that.

A tremor rippled through him. She felt it in his hand and saw it in the flicker of that ebony stare.

Yet he said nothing, *did* nothing to invite anything more.

Of course not. You just told him today you'd been harassed by your old boss.

Which meant, despite the tension she read in his face, and the hunger in his eyes, Luca was leaving it for her to decide what happened here.

If that *was* hunger in his eyes? For the first time Allegra cursed her limited experience.

Doubt wove through her. She shouldn't be doing this. Everything would change if she acted on those secret desires she'd harboured for months now.

Yet suddenly, with a fierce certainty that mocked her hesitation, Allegra knew she needed to do this.

To be true to herself.

For the past year she'd boxed herself in, enclosed herself in a narrow space where she functioned at work but had no personal life. She'd cut out the leisure activities she enjoyed, like riding a motorcycle, until this weekend.

Because Sam Parkinson had claimed it was her smiles, her vibrancy, that had lured him to attack.

He'd blamed her for what he'd done, and though that was nonsense, Allegra had taken on a load of caution, if not guilt. She'd turned herself into someone she wasn't, repressed herself, to keep safe.

For a year she'd been careful never to show she was aware of Luca as a man rather than a boss.

She was tired of pretending. Pretending to be a machine, not a woman. Pretending not to care for Luca.

She lifted her other hand and placed it along his jaw, feeling the soft brush of his short beard and the hard angle of bone beneath. He swallowed, his eyes so dark the pupils melded with ebony irises and Allegra fell into those velvet depths.

'Don't go any further, unless you're sure, Allegra.' His voice was a low burr that brushed across her skin like suede.

Sure she wanted him?

Oh, yes.

Sure she needed him, with an intensity that eclipsed anything she'd ever felt for a man?

Definitely.

Sure this was sensible?

She swallowed hard. Who knew what the future held? All she knew was that she admired Luca, liked him, desired him. That if he didn't hold her in his arms soon she'd burst. She'd put a stopper on her feelings so long. She wouldn't, couldn't put it back.

'Oh, I'm sure, Luca.'

She leaned over the arm of her chair, lifting herself so her face was right in front of his, just a breath away. Still he didn't move, but there was a coiled energy about him, like an athlete ready for the starter's gun, or an animal sighting prey, that for an instant made her hesitate.

Allegra had never done this before. Never wanted or trusted any man enough.

But deep inside she knew this was right.

She slid her hand back to spear his short, thick hair possessively. He felt so good!

There was a smile on her mouth as she closed her eyes and fitted her lips to his.

Chapter Seven

HE WAS DYING, SLOWLY DYING of torture. His whole body was in lockdown. He didn't dare move so much as a finger while Allegra sat next to him, her slim hand on his, her lovely eyes bright with enquiry and uncertainty.

The women he dated were usually confident, supremely self-assured and not at all hesitant about inviting a man into their bed.

Allegra was different in so many ways, even though he'd always thought of her as confident in her professional role.

It wasn't just looks or attitude, though they played their part. This was *Allegra*, the woman he'd appreciated and liked, but hadn't known at all. The woman who'd tormented his fantasies though he'd tried to deny it.

With her beautiful blue-grey eyes and lush mouth, she was more potently desirable than any fantasy. He smelled her: vanilla, warm female flesh and the slightest hint of musk, and his heart kicked hard into a primitive, urgent tattoo. A needy tattoo.

He wanted Allegra as he couldn't remember wanting anyone. Sitting still, not claiming her, giving her the chance to decide, was the hardest thing he could remember doing.

Then her hand was on his face, her breath warm

on him. Her fingers channelled through his hair and that touch seemed as intimate as any erotic caress. Every nerve ending danced into urgent wakefulness.

He was an inch from pulling her to him, and ending this torment, when she closed her eyes and touched her mouth to his.

The effect was electrifying, even though her kiss was gentle, almost innocent, with her lips still closed. It was enough to sever Luca's control as his blood surged south and every neuron flashed, his brain demanding more and still more.

Luca hauled her closer, pulling her over the arm of the chair and onto his lap, lashing her tight within his embrace. She was soft and curved, deliciously feminine against his granite hardness, and close wasn't enough.

Not when he anchored his hand in her fine hair, angling her head for better access. Not when she responded to the slick of his tongue along her mouth by opening her lips and letting him plunge deep.

She tasted of wine and something sweet and unfamiliar. Something that he guessed was simply Allegra. Dimly Luca registered it was a taste he'd happily grow addicted to.

Her hands wrapped over his shoulders and he dragged his palm up, over her ribcage to the swell of her breast.

She stiffened and for an instant he thought he'd scared her, but instead she arched against him, thrusting her softness into his palm. He stroked his thumb over her nipple and she moaned in the back of her throat.

He wanted to make her moan again. To scream his name in ecstasy. He wanted everything with her.

Luca deepened his kiss, mimicking the way he'd like to possess her body. And the sweetness of her response, the way she melted against him, sucking his tongue against hers, sparked wildfire in his veins.

'I want you,' he breathed, the sound lost against her mouth. But she heard. He felt the quiver right through her slender body.

She pressed closer, every part of her pure invitation. 'Then take me.'

It was as if she'd lit dynamite somewhere in his brain. He felt the silent, juddering waves of reaction roll through him, felt his hands tighten possessively on her delectable body. And he realised with shock that he was close to coming just at the sound of her words and the feel of her rounded hip against his erection.

Part of him wanted to strip her naked right here. Another part was all for simply tearing her trousers open and driving into her without niceties like undressing.

But Luca had more control than that.

Barely.

In a surge of movement he rose to his feet, cradling Allegra close in his arms, every muscle and sinew taut with aroused possessiveness.

Instantly her grip tightened, as if afraid he might drop her. Or as if she too, craved contact.

He liked that. He liked her holding onto him as if she'd never let go. And when she pulled her head back to gasp in air he liked the dazed look in her silvery eyes. It was like looking into moonlight, except there was nothing cool about Allegra's eyes. They burned with a hunger that matched his.

Swiftly, driven by the need to stamp his mark, Luca hitched her higher and bent his head, taking her mouth in a hard, proprietorial kiss. He needed to taste her again, feel that huge, trembling weight of anticipation rising up through her body to meet his.

This time when he lifted his head, she looked thoroughly kissed. Her hair was around her shoulders in glorious waves and her lips were swollen. Her eyes were diamond-bright.

For a moment they just looked at each other, both panting, trying to drag in more air. Then Allegra smiled, slowly, sending his heart spinning out of control and spurring him into action.

Luca strode across the room, through the other reception areas and towards the stairs to the executive suites where beds had been made up for them. Allegra clung close. The feel of her against him made him lope up the stairs.

Seconds later and he was swinging her to her feet beside his bed. He hadn't even taken time to turn on the light.

She swayed a little and he put out his hands to steady her. Already she felt different to his touch. Because after carrying her, after running his hands over her lithe body, he knew some of the secrets she hid beneath those boxy suits.

Anticipation licked like fire inside his belly.

'Let me undress you.' Another man might have asked. Luca demanded, his voice an unrecognisable feral growl. In the pearly light through the open curtains he saw Allegra's eyes widen but she didn't protest.

He couldn't have survived if she'd said no.

Swiftly he pushed her jacket from her shoulders, then his hands were on her shirt. He had time to register the fact Allegra enjoyed slippery silk against her skin before he tugged the garment from her shoulders and froze.

His prudish PA wore the sexiest bra he'd ever seen. Narrow ribbon straps held up lacy black cups that barely covered her nipples. With each rapid breath she took he waited for a glimpse of rosy pink.

Lust slammed into him. It would be a miracle if he lasted long enough to get a condom on! She drove him crazy and she hadn't even touched him.

It was as if she read his mind. Allegra reached out, tugging at his shirt, flicking each button undone with a single-minded precision he admired. Meanwhile he reached for the waistband of her trousers.

There was a soft gasp. Of shock? Did he imagine that her hands trembled? The idea made him pause for all of two seconds, till her exhaled breath warmed his chin and she continued with his buttons, fumbling a little now, her eyes on his shirt rather than his face.

Rapidly he undid her trousers and pushed them down her hips. When they fell Luca yanked himself free of his shirt, letting it drop to the floor.

Even in the darkened room she was enough to steal his breath.

'You are the most beautiful woman I've ever seen.' Luca raised his hand to clasp her beautiful breast, cream against black lace, then hesitated, knowing once he touched her he'd be unable to hold back. Instead he let his gaze rove from her breasts, plump above the miniscule bra, to the inward slope of her ribs down to a surprisingly small waist. Pale skin shimmered in the faint moonlight as he traced the flare of her hips then the delectable brief lacy band that passed for underwear.

Just looking at her made him feel too big for his skin.

How would it feel to touch her?

'You don't need to exaggerate, Luca.' Her voice was soft but he felt every word imprint itself on his heart.

'I'm not.' He inhaled, drawing the fragrance of her skin deep inside.

'*You're* beautiful.' She pressed a soft palm to his chest and his heart raced harder. Her other hand went to his jeans. Moments later they were undone and he was strung so tight by the feel of her knuckles brushing his skin that he feared he'd disgrace himself at any moment.

Quickly, he finished undressing and she gasped. He hoped it was in appreciation, not dismay for he'd never been more rampantly aroused. And her soft gasp merely fuelled the conflagration that was his libido. He dropped to his knees and lifted her legs from her pooling trousers, shucking her footwear at the same time.

Then, when the weight of restraint pressing down on him became unbearable, he wrapped his hands around her thighs. Slowly, savouring each delectable spot, he kissed his way from her ankles up her shins to her satiny thighs.

Allegra shifted and her breathing became uneven,

especially as he approached the strip of lace around her hips.

'Open your legs.'

There was hiss of indrawn breath, a long moment's silence, then she complied.

Luca smiled as he gently nipped her flesh through the lace. Then lower, grazing with his teeth so she shook in his hands. Holding her more firmly, he gripped the lace over one hip and dragged it down, loving the hot bloom of her skin against his mouth. Then the other side, then finally he nipped at the tiny V of lace right at her core and carefully dragged it lower.

Allegra said something far above him. It sounded like a prayer, but he couldn't hear it over the pounding of blood in his ears. He buried his face against her mound and instantly she tilted her hips towards him, offering herself for his delectation.

Using his hands now, he rolled the lace down her legs till she could step out of it. But he didn't take his eyes off the banquet before him.

He bent, licked, found the spot he sought, and heard her keen above him. Tremors racked her thighs and her fingers grabbed his head as if she was afraid she'd fall, or that he'd stop.

Luca smiled. Instead he slid a finger across the slick spot to probe deeper, then leaned in to graze his teeth across that sensitive bud. Immediately she clenched around him, drawing him tight and high as her gasp turned into a cry of pleasure. It undulated through her, wave after wave of climax, scenting the air with sex and woman, and making restraint a physical impossibility.

Rising quickly, he pushed her down onto the

bed, breaking her fall with his arm around her. Then he disengaged to search for protection in the bag beside the bed.

It was only seconds later but it seemed hours when, sheathed, he stretched out above her.

'You like it when I use my mouth?'

Allegra nodded, even in the dim light he thought he read hectic colour darkening her breasts and cheeks.

'Good.' He lowered his head and closed his teeth around her nipple, biting ever so gently. Instantly she rose off the bed, only the weight of him keeping her down.

'Luca! Please.' She cradled his head again and he almost laughed with delight that she was still so eager after that first quick climax.

'Sh.' He settled himself between her thighs and felt her heat all around him as she splayed her knees either side of his hips. Then he took her other nipple in his mouth through the lace and sucked hard.

This time her gasp was close to a scream and he could sense the heavy, beckoning throb of rapture beginning deep inside her. Allegra was glorious. So ready, so adept at pleasure. So exactly what he wanted.

Her hand inched down between them but he caught it before it reached his aching erection. He was too close to the edge to survive fondling.

'Another time,' he growled against her breast, and lifted her hand to the pillow above her head. The action arched her body delightfully up towards his mouth. With his other hand he slipped her bra undone and nudged it away so he could kiss her flesh.

But it was no good. He was too aroused. His usual repertoire of foreplay was beyond him when he had Allegra whimpering for him.

Bracing on one elbow he found her entrance and positioned himself.

Silvery eyes snared his. He felt the impact shaft through his chest as he tried to breathe. Then, without thought or technique, he moved, driving into her with one solid, powerful thrust.

There was a strange moment of hesitation, of delay, and he felt her flinch infinitesimally. But then he was sliding deeper and deeper, till he was firmly lodged right at her core.

All was stillness. He wasn't even sure he breathed. And Allegra didn't. She was still as if made of marble. But she was warm flesh and blood. Her heat sheathing him so tightly was an irresistible aphrodisiac.

He was only human. He meant to hang on, to give her pleasure after pleasure but instead found himself withdrawing then bucking again hard. And again and again.

With each movement Allegra's eyes narrowed, till all he saw was the bright glitter through lowered lashes. But her body spoke volumes. Quickly, even a little clumsily, her legs lifted to lock around his waist. Her nails dug at his shoulders and at every thrust she angled her pelvis high in welcome, her gasps becoming ever more raw.

It might have been minutes or maybe only seconds, till he registered the ripple of her muscles around him, growing in strength to a shudder then a delicious tight clamp as she came again. She called his name, making him smile until his own crisis hit with an urgency he'd never known. On and on it went, bliss and desperation making him jerk and empty himself deep within her, till there was nothing left and he collapsed, boneless, on her heaving, gorgeous body.

Chapter Eight

ALLEGRA STRETCHED, ENJOYING THE LETHARGY of wellbeing that enveloped her.

Yes, she was tender in unfamiliar places, and she suspected her throat and breasts in particular were a little red from Luca's beard, but the knowledge only made her smile. Strangely, to her surprise, even her legs felt sore.

He'd been ardent and demanding, passionate yet tender. Had he guessed it had been her first time?

She grinned and snuggled deeper beneath the cloud-soft eiderdown. She remembered the tender way he'd held her close, cocooning her in his warmth, stroking her gently, as if she were some fragile treasure instead of ordinary flesh and blood. The kisses he'd pressed to her burning skin had been heartbreakingly sweet.

Allegra had never known such peace as when she'd drifted to sleep in Luca's arms.

Then later, as fingers of pink stole across the blue peaks on the other side of the valley, she'd woken to find herself spooned against him, his arm heavy at her waist, a delicious weight. She'd been encompassed by him, the rough hair of his thighs abrading her legs, his hot, powerful chest at her back, his hand on her breast and that heavy erection… Her heart somersaulted at the memory of what he'd done with that.

He'd caressed her, drawing her from slumberous lethargy to eager abandon with a thoroughness that undid her. Only when she'd been squirming and panting in his arms, needy…no, *desperate*, did he take her.

He'd been so urgent, filling her even more than she'd imagined possible, yet she'd felt cherished, adored even. She'd loved the sound of his hoarse, broken breaths and the tell-tale quiver in those powerful hands as he'd brought her to ecstasy yet again.

His climax when it came had been a revelation. For though his expertise far outweighed hers, there'd been something about his shuddering abandon, his sheer intensity as he lost himself utterly within her, that made Allegra feel powerful and possessive. Triumphant even.

As a lover Luca was second to none.

To think she'd feared revealing her attraction! Imagine how they could have filled the empty nights before this if she'd been honest with him earlier.

But, this way at least, she knew he was attracted to the real Allegra Davis, not just to her looks. They'd worked together so long their relationship was founded on trust and respect. She'd already known so much about him before last night, and even though she'd hidden a lot from him, he knew her better than practically anyone.

A sound made her look up. There in the doorway, stood Luca, a tray in his hands. His damp hair was brushed back off his face and he wore denims and a black T shirt. A strange little jitter of excitement started down between her legs and travelled up through her body. After just one night her body associated him with sexual arousal. And satisfaction.

But the smell of fresh coffee made her nostrils twitch and her stomach growl.

He smiled and crossed the room, putting the tray on the bedside table. Despite the last twenty-four hours, Allegra wasn't used to seeing him in anything but business clothes. She couldn't take her eyes off him. He looked good enough to eat.

His eyebrows rose and he chuckled, the sound like rich, dark chocolate lapping along her veins. 'I'd be happy to oblige except we won't be alone much longer.'

Heat bloomed in Allegra's face as she realised she'd spoken aloud. But it was a little late for embarrassment. Besides, she *wanted* the opportunity to explore that potently masculine body at her own pace.

Her gaze dropped to the zipper on his faded jeans and her interest in coffee disintegrated.

Till he sat on the side of the bed, cupped a hand around her jaw and kissed her with such ruthless thoroughness that she lost her train of thought.

When she swam back to reality he was propping pillows behind her back, then lifting her up to lean against them, his hands roving and caressing along the way. Allegra wriggled and tugged at the sheet that had got caught around her leg. She winced as she shifted, her leg protesting the sudden movement. It hadn't hurt like that last night. Clearly the painkiller had worn off.

Luca frowned then ripped the sheet away and swore, his gaze fixed on her leg.

From ankle to thigh ran a dark bruise where she'd hit the gravel on the side of the road yesterday. Funny how it had barely been tender when she'd made love with him. Just now her leg had been stiff but not nearly as much as she'd expect from a bruise so vivid and vast.

'That must hurt like the devil.' His voice was grim. 'I'm sorry. I should have realised.'

'No.' Allegra closed her hand around his. 'I didn't realise either.' And neither of them had seen the damage to her leg last night. 'I'm fine, truly.' But even as she spoke pain tingled the length of her leg. It was as if, in the cold light of day, her body insisted on making the injury obvious. Last night she'd been buoyed on an ecstatic wave of excitement and pleasure. Now she was mortal again.

The sudden silence was broken by the rev of an engine approaching the resort. Not one engine, but two, she realised.

'The workmen,' Luca said, his eyes still on her leg, his brow puckered into a scowl.

'What time is it?' Suddenly she realised how very bright the light was. She'd overslept, but who could blame her?

'Don't worry about it. Just relax and enjoy your breakfast.' Those dark eyes lifted to hers and the intensity of his stare snagged her breath. Even her silly heart fluttered.

She breathed in, trying to centre herself and instead inhaled the fresh, unadulterated scent of Luca. Excitement trembled through her, swirling lower and lower to settle deep in her pelvis.

Oh, she had it bad.

He wasn't kissing her or whispering outrageously sexy comments in her ear. He wasn't even touching her anymore yet her heart was battering her ribs in eagerness. Not just for his touch but for everything about him. His attention, his passion, his quirky sense of humour, his tender consideration and impatience, his delight in her body and his understanding of so much she'd shared about herself.

Because you love him.

You've loved him almost from the start. You just didn't let yourself believe anything could come of it so you pretended it wasn't real.

Suddenly it all made sense. Even her enthusiasm for working late into the night when Luca was finalising a new project. Because she knew he relied on her and she didn't want to let him down.

The air rushed from her lungs in a puff of astonishment. At the same time her chest expanded, filling with a warm, unfamiliar glow as unstoppable joy rose.

She loved him!

'Luca—' She put her hand on his arm, not knowing exactly what she was going to say, but before she could continue he was on his feet, his expression surprisingly stern.

'I'd better go and head them off before they come looking for me.' His gaze flickered back to her leg and his frown deepened. Allegra dragged the sheet over herself, feeling abruptly naked in a way she hadn't last night.

How silly was that?

'No time even for coffee with me?' She looked at the two cups on the tray. Okay, so there was no time for him to come back to bed, but, with the sudden knowledge of her feelings, wonderful, scary and overwhelming, she needed another of his smiles.

Love was such a big thing. She needed reassurance, even if she had no intention of sharing her feelings just yet.

Luca reached for the cup and drained it in one swallow. When he put it down, his expression bordered on grim.

'Sorry, no. Take your time, Allegra. Rest, then bathe. I can manage here.' He nodded and turned away.

Nodded! Just as if they were back in the office and he was giving her instructions – boss to PA.

What about a kiss? Even one of those bone-melting smiles?

He paused at the door and her heart banged her ribs. *Now* he'd smile. Her lips curved up in anticipation and she wrapped her arms around herself, nursing secret pleasure.

But when he turned back he looked, not at her, but at a point between her and the tray. 'Take the day off. We did most of what needed to be done yesterday. I'll finish up here and you head back to Milan. In fact,' he dragged his phone from his back pocket, 'I'll arrange a car to take you back. You won't want to ride the bike when you're stiff and sore.'

Allegra was glad for her crossed arms. They imparted a little warmth to a body that turned glacially cold. On the surface his words were thoughtful but the way he refused to look at her, and the fact he was sending her away...

Distress climbed her spine like icy, numbing fingertips.

'I'd rather stay. I can—'

'No.' His eyes met hers and she felt a discordant jangling of nerves, then he looked away. 'It's better that you go back to Milan. There's no need for you to stay. I'll see you in the city.'

Allegra sank back against the fluffy pillows. It shouldn't feel like a rebuff. She knew he was going to see his family after the site visit. She surely didn't expect him to invite her to meet his relatives simply because they'd spent the night together?

Did she?

Of course not. Yet she'd expected more than coffee and an order to return to Milan.

She'd thought they could spend more time together.

Yeah, making love while the place is filled with workmen. As if!

But at least a smile, another cuddle.

She opened her mouth to say something, so needy in her newly-identified feelings, that she had to have more – a tender word, anything.

Before she could speak he was out the door and she was left behind, listening to it snick shut after him.

Silence.

Nothing but the hammer of her pulse in her ears and the hoarse gasp of her indrawn breath.

She reminded herself he was protecting her from prying eyes, heading off the workmen before they came to the bedroom wing. But it felt as if they were back in the office, he giving orders and she obeying.

No, not quite. Over the months they'd developed a rapport and Luca treated her as a colleague whose opinion he valued, not a robot to comply with his every whim. There'd been none of the rapport just now.

Because he'd read the feelings she hadn't been able to hide?

Because, despite his kindness in bringing coffee, he wasn't interested in more than a single night?

He'd looked at her bruised leg and something had changed. But what? Had he been reminded of yesterday? What they'd been to each other before she kissed him? Of their lives outside this place? Maybe Luca had simply responded to her neediness last night but in the clear light of day couldn't bring himself to continue a liaison with his PA.

Allegra had seen the women he took out – gorgeous, leggy blondes with megawatt smiles and golden skin. Women who hung on his words and presumably deferred to his every whim. Not like his conscientious assistant who could be relied on to ask the difficult questions no-one else would.

She reached out and took the coffee in fingers that trembled. Surely she was reading too much into this. Luca had a lot on his mind. Things would be fine, better than fine, when she saw him next.

Except when she saw him next, Luca was in conversation with the project manager. And in addition to the workmen finalising the sun deck, there was an army of decorators delivering curtains.

'Luca.' She was proud of her voice. Light, warm, not at all clingy.

Instantly he turned, his eyes zeroing in on her, warming her from her scalp to her soles. No, that connection hadn't disappeared. It had intensified if anything.

He said something to the manager and crossed to her, frowning as he took in her motorcycle leathers.

'There's a car coming—'

'I cancelled it. The bike's okay so I'll ride it. I'll take my time since I'm not due in the office till tomorrow. Of course,' she paused, smiling, her voice low, 'I could stay here a little longer to help.'

Ask me to stay.

Ask me to stay. Smile at me. Better yet, touch me. Just your hand on mine would be enough. So I know—

'No. I'd prefer it if you headed back and got some rest.' His brow wrinkled in a frown. 'I'll arrange another car. A local driver so you don't have to wait for a car from Milan. And I'll organise transport for the bike.'

Then he smiled. Not the smouldering, devil-in-his-eyes smile that had stolen her heart but the perfunctory expression of a busy man ticking off an item on a packed agenda. 'I'll see you back in the city.' He paused, his hand lifting, and she thought he was going to pull her close. But a couple of decorators crossed the room towards them, their arms full of curtains, and the moment was lost.

The project manager approached, his gaze curious as he took in her leather gear, but he turned to Luca with some query Allegra didn't hear.

The bustle went on around her and, with one last look, Luca turned away. Allegra was left wondering how delight and excitement could morph so quickly to dust and cold.

She turned on her heel and strode to the bedroom. She wouldn't wait for someone to drive her.

If she couldn't be with Luca, and clearly he didn't want her around, then she'd rather be alone.

Chapter Nine

'Morning, Allegra.' Luca strode into the office, a deliberately casual tone to his voice. 'How are you feeling today? Any after effects from the accident?'

It had been incredibly difficult, returning to Milan last night without going straight to her apartment to check on her. But guilt, like a claw gripping his vitals, had stopped him.

He'd done wrong and he owed her some distance. Besides, Allegra was sensible enough to seek medical assistance if she needed it. Not that that had convinced him through a long, sleepless night.

She turned from the table where she'd been positioning a bowl of fresh flowers.

Luca's heart slammed his ribs then limped on, picking up speed till it raced full-tilt.

He'd told himself he'd imagined this desperate, all-consuming desire. Surely it hadn't been as overwhelming as he remembered. But here, now, looking into Allegra's wary, breathtakingly beautiful face, he realised imagination hadn't embroidered a thing.

The impulse to go to her, to wrap her tight in his arms and check for himself that she was okay was almost unstoppable.

'Apart from a bruise I'm perfectly fine.' Her lips

turned up in the brief, noncommittal smile he remembered from her first weeks in the office. It was nothing like the dazzling smiles she'd given him in the Alps.

Disappointment drilled his belly.

What had he expected? That she'd greet him with open arms after he sent her away? He only had himself to blame. But the fact was, even knowing he'd done wrong, he hadn't trusted himself to touch her again, kiss her as he'd wanted, and then withdraw to give her space.

Luca took in the tightly pulled-back hair and familiar bulky suit, his gaze lingering on those glorious eyes, no longer camouflaged by heavy glasses, and that ripe, lust-inducing mouth.

He wanted her. Here. Now. Stretched across the table, or up against the wall, or sitting astride him on the swivel chair that was all that stood between them.

'You're not sore?'

A flicker of something crossed Allegra's features and she darted a look to the door he'd closed behind him, as if worried others would hear. Faint colour scored her cheeks and Luca plunged his hands deep in his pockets rather than trace the heat under her satiny skin.

'My leg's a bit stiff but that's all.' The blush intensified and Luca realised she was thinking of other places she'd probably been sore after their loving.

Instant recall of her voluptuous body welcoming him, of her sighs and kisses, and her tight heat, had his blood drumming too fast.

Another reason for guilt.

She'd been a virgin! Unbelievable but true. He'd

taken her innocence, only realising too late that he should have been gentler. And when he did realise, did he hold back? No, he'd been voracious for her delectable body. He'd persuaded her to accept his caresses again and again, purely because he couldn't get enough of her.

But that was only one item on his conscience's list of failings.

She'd been harassed sexually by her boss and clearly mistrusted men. He should never have made a move while he was in a position of authority over her.

Even if she didn't have that troubled history, sex between co-workers was a recipe for disaster. He *never* crossed that line.

Perhaps worst of all, she'd been in an accident just hours before. He told himself she'd known what she was doing, inviting his kisses. But was it true?

The fact was he'd taken advantage of a woman who might, for all he knew, have been concussed, not thinking straight. Maybe she'd simply needed comfort and he'd abused her innocence. Why else would she give away her virginity so readily, when she'd guarded it into her mid-twenties?

He wanted to think it was because she'd felt that irresistible link between them too, but dismissed that as vanity.

He'd told himself that she'd wanted him. He'd brushed aside everything else, even the memory of her bike sliding sideways towards the cliff. Until the morning when he'd seen the bruising and reality had collapsed on top of him. In all his thirty-four years he'd never felt such guilt.

His insides twisted as shame, like a rusty blade, ploughed his belly.

Instead of a duty of care, all he'd worried about was his own carnal appetites.

'Was there anything else?' Her hands gripped the back of the chair before her, and despite her calm face, Luca read her tension.

Hell! Was she nervous, being with him? The idea was unbearable.

'Yes, there is, actually.' He breathed deep and pushed back his shoulders. 'Give me a minute then come into my office. We need to talk.' He had to do the decent thing.

Even if it was too little, too late.

We need to talk. It sounded almost like a threat. Not the words of a lover.

But he wasn't her lover now, was he? He hadn't embraced her or kissed her or even smiled. Instead Luca was all business.

Was that all it had been? Her glorious night of love? A few hours respite from the business that ruled Luca's life?

Allegra thought she couldn't feel any worse than she already did, watching the man who'd taken her to such rapturous heights treat her like a polite stranger. But she'd been wrong. Pain wrung her insides, making her gasp.

Could she have been so wrong about Luca? Had she given her affection, and herself, to a man who wasn't capable of caring? She thought she'd seen past the businessman to the passionate, tender, exciting man beneath the suit.

Maybe she'd been totally wrong. Maybe he didn't care.

Oh, there'd been the call soon after she arrived in the city, when her heart had leapt with hope. But he'd simply been concerned to check if she'd got there safely since she'd spurned the car he ordered. There'd been no soft, whispered words. No promise to meet her as soon as he returned to Milan. Nothing personal.

And it didn't seem like there'd be anything personal now.

Grabbing her notebook, she straightened her jacket and headed for his office. It took every scrap of self-respect she could conjure to keep her face bland. She refused to abase herself by begging for his attention. Even if she wanted nothing more than to throw herself into Luca's arms and beg him to love her, physically and emotionally.

The man who'd just walked into the office was *not* the man she'd given herself to in the Dolomites.

Allegra swallowed hard. Whatever hopes she'd held onto that their night had been special for him too had withered in the last five minutes.

Luca wasn't behind the desk but silhouetted against the window so she couldn't read his expression. Allegra slipped into a chair before the desk, not trusting her shaky knees.

'You wanted to talk?' She kept the snap out of her voice, just, but the sudden hitch of his shoulders told her he heard…something.

Good. Then he'd realise she was no pushover. Even if she'd been outrageously needy for him the other night.

'Yes.' He folded his arms but didn't approach the

desk. He cleared his throat and for an instant she wondered if he was nervous. But that couldn't be. Luca juggled multi-billion dollar deals, negotiating with some of the world's most powerful investors. *She* wouldn't make him nervous.

Finally he strode across to the desk and sat down, facing her. She'd never seen him look so grim, long lines curving around his mouth and a frown marring his brow.

'The other night,' he began then paused when she stiffened.

'The other night was wonderful. You're a generous, passionate, special woman, Allegra.'

His words stalled and she found herself wondering how words of praise could sound like goodbye. But that's what they did. There was a ruthless finality about the tone of his voice, his guarded stare and taut body, that was unmistakeable.

'And?' She lifted her chin, meeting his eyes.

Luca was the first to look away. 'And despite that, it should never have happened that way.' Pain jabbed her chest and her breath stopped. 'I have to apologise, Allegra. I took advantage of you. For that I'm very sorry.' Swiftly his gaze lifted, skewering her where she sat.

He was *apologising* for giving her the most wonderful, exciting, emotionally rewarding experience of her life?

Emotional for her. Clearly not for him. Hadn't she known her feelings weren't reciprocated?

She pursed her lips, wondering how she could still feel weak with love for Luca when he was giving her the brush off. The trouble was, now she'd let that genie out of the bottle, there was no pushing it back in.

She didn't just desire Luca. She'd fallen in love with him. And suddenly their night together took on the dimensions of one giant mistake. Because she feared she'd never be able to hide her emotions as she once had. He'd got too close to her, in so many ways.

Luca's heart sank. Allegra looked stricken.

'I'm sorry. I—'

'For goodness sake, stop apologising.'

There was a definite snap in her voice as suddenly she came alive. More like the daredevil bike rider he'd met in the mountains than the mousy PA who'd shared his office so long. Her eyes shone bright and her pallor receded as her cheeks bloomed rose pink. His heart skipped a beat as relief flooded him. He hated seeing her look so lost.

'It was just a night, after all.'

'Pardon?' Luca wasn't used to being on the back foot but he had a sudden compelling certainty he'd missed something vital.

She waved one hand, a couple of pretty enamelled bangles tinkling at her wrist. Since when had Allegra worn jewellery? He'd never seen so much as a chain around her neck.

'You look so guilty,' she murmured. 'It wasn't the end of the world, surely? You took precautions. I'm not going to corner you with an unwanted pregnancy and try to blackmail you into marriage.'

Luca shook his head, trying to get his head around her attitude. She didn't sound like the injured woman. Or the sheltered virgin he'd mentally beaten himself up for seducing.

'I never thought for a moment you'd do anything like that.'

Though part of his brain was still stuck on the idea of Allegra pregnant with his child. His attention dropped to her breasts and lower. He remembered the velvety softness of her belly and his fingers twitched as he imagined stroking her there when she was rounded and taut with his baby.

A visceral possessiveness flooded him. He wasn't in a hurry for children, or for a wife. Yet the idea of shackling Allegra to him with a brood of kids held an appallingly potent appeal.

Luca blinked, trying to clear his head.

'Good, then we're agreed there's no harm done.' She sounded like a chairman, wrapping up a divisive boardroom discussion. Strange, he was the one who habitually took that role.

'Harm?' He was too flummoxed by unfamiliar feelings to know if there'd been any harm. But he couldn't insult her by saying that. 'I just want you to know I'm sorry. I shouldn't have—'

Again she cut him off with a wave of her hand. 'Don't say any more. There's no need.'

Luca should be thanking his lucky stars she was taking this so well, but it wasn't at all how he'd imagined her responding. Apologies were rare in his world. He prided himself on doing the decent thing whenever possible. His pride rankled that she made so little of it.

'Well, if that's all, I need to go. I've got to finalise the report for your nine o'clock video conference.'

No, that wasn't all. He felt like he'd barely begun.

'Are you sure you're up to being at work?' That had haunted him all last night. Worry about those injuries still hounded him. Guilt that he should have cared for her, not caved in to temptation.

'I already told you. I'm fine.'

She didn't look it, but he knew enough of women to keep his tongue still. Oh, she was beautiful, but the shadows in her eyes and the way she held her mouth betrayed stress.

The trouble was, he was used to dating women who were happy to enjoy sex without strings.

None of the De Laurentis brothers ever had trouble attracting women. And when there were so many willing women, where was the incentive to do anything other than play the field? Of them all, only Matteo had committed himself to a woman and look where that had ended. Luca's second brother was separated, unhappily so.

Though now Luca thought about it, Gennaro, besotted with his fashion designer, Chiara, had looked supremely pleased with himself last time they'd caught up.

Now, for the first time, Luca found himself wanting more from a woman. He wanted sex with Allegra, but he wanted her to be happy. He wanted to care for her, and make her laugh too, as they'd laughed together in the mountains. But he had no clue how to go about that when she was putting on her brisk, office persona. He saw it now, like a cloak covering the vibrant woman he'd finally discovered.

He could seduce her here in the office, ignoring propriety and caution. He didn't like it that she acted as if nothing important had happened. It was a defence mechanism, he knew, but it irked. Especially as their night together had marked him to his very core.

'Right. I'll get that report to you, with coffee, within fifteen minutes.'

Silently Luca watched her leave, a whirlwind of efficiency, and pondered how on earth he was going to connect with the real Allegra again. He'd been certain she'd expect far more than a one night stand. Was that bruised ego dictating his thoughts? Or something more profound?

Restless, he stalked to the window to stare at the building city traffic.

He'd give her time, he decided. He wouldn't push, *yet*. He'd respect her space for a few days so she knew he didn't intend to try forcing her into anything. Then he'd suggest they continue their affair, discreetly, so she didn't feel self-conscious before the other staff. He'd send flowers to her home. Invite her to dinner. Or better yet, a romantic weekend away.

Luca smiled, feeling better already. He hated not being in control. Now he had a plan to fine tune. A plan to persuade Allegra back into his bed.

All he needed was patience.

Chapter Ten

'THE MEETING IS TAKING LONGER than I expected.' Luca's tone was businesslike but even over the phone his deep voice did calamitous things to Allegra's insides. She pressed a hand to her stomach and took a deep breath, silently berating herself for reacting. 'I won't make it back from Rome today. You'd better email that contract to me so I can look at it tonight.'

Allegra's mouth tightened. She should have been in Rome with Luca for the negotiations. She was always at his side when he finalised major deals. But not this week. Not since they'd made love in the mountains and she'd touched heaven, only to return to earth with a jarring thud to discover her world had changed for the worse.

Not her world, but Luca.

He kept her at a distance, clearly regretting the intimacy they'd shared. Not just physically but professionally too, as if he wasn't comfortable working with her now.

Almost as bad, he treated her like some breakable, porcelain doll, insisting she stay in Milan instead of travel with him. Chasing her out of the office early while he worked on, as if he thought she couldn't hack the pace of work anymore.

Or, more probably, he just doesn't want to be alone

with you again.

He's uncomfortable. Normally he doesn't have to face ex-lovers in the cold hard light of day when he's finished with them. But he's stuck with you.

If anything the stilted atmosphere between them grew worse as the days progressed. Gone was their camaraderie, the give and take, the closeness. A different closeness to sex but one she valued just as much.

Pain scored her heart at what she'd lost.

'I'll send it right away. Is there anything else, Luca?' Deliberately, she let her voice lower and soften over his name, turning it into a caress.

Who was she trying to torment? Him? As if to remind him what he was missing? Or herself, for not being able to put that night behind her?

She stiffened, hurrying on before he could answer. 'The costed plan and VIP guest list for the grand opening party at the Thai resort have arrived. I'll send them to you as well.'

'Excellent.' But he didn't sound pleased. He sounded distracted. Or maybe annoyed. She'd spent days hiding her pain and disappointment behind what she'd hoped was perfect professionalism. But perhaps that professionalism bordered too close to snarky impatience.

'Allegra?'

'Yes?' Her heart crashed against her ribs. He didn't sound businesslike now. Whatever he was about to say, this was personal. She could tell, even from a distance of nearly six hundred kilometres.

'Cancel my appointment for lunch tomorrow. I'll be back in Milan then and we need to talk.'

Talk? Like when he'd told her sleeping with her

had been a mistake?

Allegra sagged back in her leather chair and stared at the lush, richly patterned wallpaper the decorator had used to give the outer office a warm feel. She felt warm now. Burning up, in fact.

With anger?

Or impatience with herself for not having this out with him earlier? To her disgust, she'd come back to Milan and fallen into the role of quiescent underling instead of fighting for what she wanted.

Now, finally, after days pretending nothing had happened between them, of cutting her off when she tried to talk with him, finally Luca was ready to discuss it. To clear the air, of course. The tension in the office had ratcheted higher each day. It couldn't be ignored any longer.

'I'll order lunch in and—'

'No.' He cut her off. 'I'll arrange something.'

She'd love to believe he had a romantic lunch for two in mind, but he was back to brusque now, his tone clipped and determined. She knew that tone. It was the voice of a man who'd made a decision and couldn't wait to act on it. Luca always moved quickly once he made his mind up.

What had he decided? To offer her an affair? Or tell her they couldn't go on working like this?

'Allegra, are you still there?' No mistaking his impatience this time.

'Of course.' She breathed deep and swivelled her chair to look out the window. As if mirroring her mood, the day had turned slate grey, rain pounding down relentlessly.

It was the complete opposite of the intoxicating clear blue sky in the mountains. But *that* was fantasy, she reminded herself. *This* was reality.

'I'll see you tomorrow then.' She forced herself back into the role of ever-efficient PA. 'And I've been working on the Venice report. I'll have it ready for tomorrow too.'

She heard someone in the background, speaking to Luca. His meeting must be resuming. 'Good. I'll see you then.'

The connection went dead and Allegra grimaced as she put the phone down. Had she really expected lover-like warmth from him? If so, if she'd secretly harboured a hope he felt more for her than he'd let on, any such hope must be dead now.

Maybe that accounted for the strange tightness banding her chest.

She shoved her chair back and rose to pace the office. She'd see what tomorrow brought. And after that…

Well, she'd face that when the time came.

But tomorrow didn't bring illumination. It didn't even bring Luca. She got a text saying he'd been held up but he'd see her in the office when he arrived.

Noon became one, then two, then three. By four pm Allegra could take no more. She marched from his office to hers, tidying, straightening, trying to work off some of her excess energy without success. Everything was up to date and all she could do now was wait for Luca to arrive.

She caught sight of her reflection in the window and stalled. Had she really hoped Luca would relent and say he wanted to be with her? Surely that's why she wore this brand new, sleeveless jersey dress that swung round her thighs as she walked and ended just above her knees. She'd bought it in a flash of defiance, telling herself she could dress as she pleased now he knew who she really was.

But the insidious truth was that she'd dressed in hopes of piquing his interest. Of making him see her once more as a desirable woman.

Pain beat through her, a terrible reverberation that pummelled her bones and made even her teeth ache.

Fool! You love him. You loved him before and sex with him just made those stupid romantic imaginings seem possible. But they're not.

He couldn't have made it any clearer that you were simply an itch he wanted to scratch. A curiosity to be savoured. But now he's regretting the night you spent together.

All week she'd tortured herself, imagining heat in those fathomless dark eyes, desire in his suddenly rigid body when she drew too close.

But she couldn't fool herself anymore. She'd done that too long.

He just doesn't want you, Allegra. Face it!

If he did, he'd have told her, shown her, before now.

As for this discussion they were supposed to have…

She shivered as she recalled his deep, serious tone. It was something momentous, she was sure of that. And if it wasn't that he wanted to pursue a relationship with her, it had to be that he'd decided she was an embarrassment he didn't want to face in the office each day.

Oh, he wouldn't sack her. Luca had too much integrity for that. But he'd offer her work somewhere else in his global company. Somewhere they didn't have to meet daily.

Allegra folded her arms over her chest and hugged tight, holding back the hot emotions threatening to spill out.

The question was – what would she do about it? Would she meekly follow his lead?

She'd spent the last twelve months bruised and hiding her real self because of the actions of one man. A man who'd made her feel, despite all logic, that she was in some way to blame for the way he'd hit on her. She'd penned herself into a half-life she didn't want anymore. She needed more. She wanted the freedom to be *herself*. Whether it meant wearing cute dresses or riding a motorbike or going to bed with a man she loved.

Her defiance wavered and her chin wobbled before she set it high.

She loved Luca but he didn't love her. No amount of courage could fix that. But at least she could decide her own future on her own terms. She didn't have to wait meekly for him to dictate how it would be.

Luca loped up the stairs in his Milan headquarters, ignoring the plush lift. He needed to work off some of the tension dragging at his shoulders.

It had been a hellish day. His morning meeting had pushed to two then three hours as negotiations grew more convoluted. He'd wanted this deal, badly. But finally he'd shoved back his chair and declared to a room full of stunned lawyers that the deal was off.

He had other priorities. Namely the woman waiting in their shared executive suite. Just the thought of her made his pulse pound and his breath quicken.

How he'd kept his hands to himself these last few days, he didn't know. But he'd been determined to show her he didn't expect to use his position as her boss to force her into his bed again. Even though that was exactly where he wanted her.

His belly tightened and his breath quickened at the memory of her naked in his arms.

He'd been aching for her so long and today had turned into a nightmare, where the quicker he tried to reach her, the slower he moved.

First a problem with air traffic control in Rome. Then a mechanical difficulty with the plane. Then the realisation he'd forgotten to charge his phone, and left the charger in his Rome apartment.

Finally he'd grabbed another phone and rung the office but hadn't been able to reach Allegra. She must have been in a meeting and he wasn't in the mood for speaking with one of the junior staff, who'd pick up if she didn't answer immediately. Six times he'd tried and each time his frustration grew. It did no good to tell himself she'd have answered instantly if she'd recognised his number calling.

But now he was here. Relief settled on his bones as he shoved open the door to the executive suite. He strode in, and found it empty.

'Allegra?' He scowled and looked at his watch. Far too early for her to have left, even on a Friday.

He crossed the room and stared at her empty desk. She was always tidy and efficient, but the bare, gleaming wood looked too blank. Her computer was off too.

'Allegra?' He put his head into the kitchen they shared but it was empty.

Pulse quickening, he headed for his office. She'd said she had reports for him. She'd be in there, waiting.

He had a moment's irrepressible vision of her waiting, perched on his desk in nothing but the ultra-brief, black lace underwear she'd worn last week. All that creamy smooth skin on display and her beautiful ebony hair spilling in waves around her shoulders.

Somehow the sexy underwear was all the more seductive on a woman like Allegra who didn't dress to attract a man.

Palm to the door, he pushed it open and marched in, anticipation sharp on his tongue.

Empty. There was no-one there.

His heart smashed against his ribs in a brutal rhythm of frustration and, yes, worry. It wasn't like Allegra to leave his office unattended.

Then he saw the paper on his desk. Dead centre. Unmissable. He didn't know why but everything inside him stopped, as if his heart forgot to beat.

He strode across and snatched it up.

It was typed, but signed by Allegra with a slashing, purposeful signature.

Luca read and reread the brief note. But there was no misinterpreting the message. His stalwart assistant, the woman who'd burrowed under all his defences and surprised him into the realisation that he wanted not just sex but a serious relationship, had resigned.

Chapter Eleven

ALLEGRA SLICKED ON HER NEW lipstick and immediately felt better. After a year of wearing clear gloss it was a treat to dress up. Subtle makeup made the most of her eyes – eyes she'd spent far too long hiding. And now a rich, warm lipstick to complement her colouring.

She angled her head, taking in her reflection, and smiled, ignoring the fact it was crooked and a little wobbly. Determined, she thrust aside the disappointment and hurt. If she let herself dwell on that she'd be huddled on the floor of the executive bathroom, a blubbering mess.

Allegra intended to leave the office with her head high and her armour fully in place.

So what if Luca hadn't been bothered keeping his appointment with her? So what if he avoided her? That he didn't value her, much less care for her?

Her world didn't have to revolve around Luca de Laurentis. No matter how much she'd let it.

She was young and fit and capable. She'd get over this. She'd got over what had happened in London and she'd move past this too.

Except in London no-one had bruised your heart.

Bruised, she told herself. Not broken.

If she said it often enough it might turn out to

be true. Or at least she could pretend it was. And if she really didn't feel like going out on the town, visiting one of the lively bars the girls on the floor below frequented, well, she'd try to enjoy herself when she got there. It would do her good to be with people other than Luca.

Allegra blinked and swallowed hard. It felt like someone had lined her throat with sandpaper.

She refused to let pain triumph. She was *not* going to hand in her notice and slink straight home to sob out her woes. It would probably come to that later tonight, but it was important for her self-respect that she at least pretended to be strong. Pretended to be heart whole.

Her lips twisted as she took in her reflection. In a couple of deft moves she pulled her hair down so it spilled across her shoulders and bare upper arms. But it had been too long since she'd gone out wearing it free. Instead she compromised, pinning it back up loosely, so a few strands framed her face and her natural waves added body to the style.

She tilted her chin. It didn't matter that she felt bruised all over by Luca's patent discomfort, being with her now they'd shared a bed. It didn't matter that she was walking away from a job she loved. What mattered was taking care of herself. Moving on and finding a life that was right for her.

No more camouflage.

No more tiptoeing around men and their egos.

In fact — no more men!

Now, there was something she'd drink to. It was early but she'd be happy to raise a glass of chilled prosecco to that toast.

One last glance told her she'd left nothing behind.

She closed her bag, took a deep breath and walked out into the office.

And straight into a solid wall of heat, muscle and finely woven wool suiting.

Allegra gasped. And with the oxygen came a waft of all-too-familiar spice and man scent. A pair of large hands clamped her upper arms, holding her firmly against that tall body and her head rocked back. Instantly she was lost in the velvet darkness of his eyes.

'Luca!' Emotion pummelled her. Excitement, pleasure, and then the inevitable pain. He wasn't here for *her*. This was his office.

Now she'd decided to resign, it would have been far easier not to see him again. Especially as her body was already responding so flagrantly. Her nipples hardened, pressing into her bra and there was a soft heat at the apex of her thighs that told its own story.

Mentally she'd accepted that he wasn't for her, that it had all been a ridiculous, painful fantasy to think they could ever be a couple. But physically she was still in thrall to him.

'Allegra! I thought you'd gone.' There was a raw rasp to his deep voice, a desperate note that made her stare.

If only she *had* gone, instead of trying to talk herself into an evening of socialising when all she wanted was to cry her heart out.

No, not *all* she wanted. Standing rammed up against his hard frame, she admitted she still wanted Luca. Would possibly always want him. And wasn't that just pathetic?

If only she'd walked out of the office as soon as

she'd typed her resignation!

'I'm just on my way now.' She stepped back, except his hands stopped her, tightening on her. She felt the imprint of those long fingers on the bare skin of her upper arms. It was enough to make a woman wish she'd worn a long-sleeved suit instead of this new, lightweight dress.

'Not yet.' His jaw hardened and she read the tic of a pulse in his temple. Surely it raced too fast? Almost as fast as her own runaway heart?

With the last shreds of pride she cut the connection between them, glancing down at her watch.

'I'm afraid I'm running late.'

'For a job interview? Or a date?' The rough urgency of his tone had her lifting her head, taking in the combative set of his jaw and the scowl he wore. This was Luca as she'd rarely seen him. He looked on the edge of control.

A tremor of excitement mingled with foreboding rippled down her spine.

'That's none of your business, Luca.' She firmed her lips, hating the melting sensation along her bones when she tasted his name on her tongue. Ridiculous, but it made her think of the taste of him in her mouth, richly addictive.

His hands tightened and he thrust his face forward into her space. 'Of course it is. You work for me. You're my—'

'Your what, Luca?' She stiffened. How dare he act so possessively? He'd all but ignored her this week. It was clear that their night together, far from heralding a new stage in their relationship, had made him uncomfortable working with her. 'Your reliable PA? Well, PAs can resign and I have.

There's a letter on your desk.'

'I've seen it.' He spoke through clenched teeth, the sound emerging as a low, feral growl that warned he was close to losing his cool.

Good! She'd hate to think he felt nothing at all about her leaving. In fact she hoped he had incredible difficulty finding a replacement for her.

'Excellent.' She raised her shoulders. 'Now if you'd just let me go.'

'No!' Instead of releasing her he stepped closer, forcing her back a pace. 'I won't let you go. What the *hell* do you think you're doing, leaving me that snippy little note?'

Allegra looked up into his darkly handsome face and wished that for once she wouldn't react. That she could survey him as coolly as she did any other man. To her horror she couldn't. Even now. Even with a belly full of righteous indignation and a determination to save herself by walking away.

'You're hurting me,' she lied, but it was worth it when he released his hold and stepped back. When he touched her… She shut her eyes. Surely one day she'd no longer react to him this way.

'What's going on, Allegra?' His voice was soft but husky as if he had trouble controlling it.

See how she imagined things even now? Because deep down part of her still wanted to believe the magic they'd shared might last.

She snapped her eyes open and took one last look at his glorious, hard, beautiful face. As if she needed to fix the memory! She feared his features were already permanently engraved in her brain.

She sidestepped to walk past him but he blocked her. When she turned the other way he stepped in front of her again. He looked large and implacable and determined to get his own way.

Tough!

'It was not a snippy note. It was a perfectly reasonable resignation.'

'As if we're complete strangers!' He raked his hand back through his hair leaving him looking just rumpled enough to evoke memories of him in bed.

Allegra slammed the door on that train of thought. 'No, we *were* boss and employee, which is why I offered a resignation. I'd prefer not to work off my notice since I've got so much leave accrued, but of course—'

'There is no *of course*,' he said with a gritted control that told her a volcano of fury simmered just below the surface.

'In the circumstances I think it best to leave.'

Before her eyes the colour washed from his face, leaving his features pale and starkly defined. 'You think I'll use my position as your employer to harass you sexually?'

'No! Of course not. You're nothing like my old boss.' Luca had never pressed unwanted attentions on her, or on anyone else. The problem was his attentions were all too welcome, but he just wasn't interested. And she had no intention of putting herself through hell, working for a man she loved, who didn't care for her.

The fact he'd even consider it for a moment flummoxed her. 'You know what happened between us wasn't like that. And here in the office you've never once...' She shrugged, her voice petering out. How badly she'd wanted him to take up where they'd left off.

'So what is it? Why leave, like *that*.'

She could almost imagine that was hurt in his tone. Maybe she'd dented his pride?

Allegra pressed a hand to her temple, her thoughts in turmoil. What did he want from her? Blood?

'Why the third degree? I thought you'd be glad. You're obviously uncomfortable working with me now. You barely talk to me, you don't take me to meetings and most of the time you can barely look me in the eye.' She jammed her hands on her hips and stared him down, even though he was so much taller.

Except instead of looking guilty, she saw colour wash his taut features again and his eyes gleam as if with excitement. 'You thought I didn't want to work with you anymore?'

'It's obvious. You send me home early, you stop me attending the meeting in Rome for the deal I've sweated blood for. I'll have you know I worked every bit as hard as you did to pull that deal off.' Righteous anger ripped through her veins, but it wasn't enough to counter the wilting inside. Any minute now she'd reveal her true feelings. She was just too close to the edge.

'Let me leave, Luca. I've had enough.'

To her relief, and horror, he backed away a pace, giving her freedom to walk past him.

Allegra swallowed convulsively, knowing this, finally, was goodbye.

She took a step, then another, keeping her chin up and her eyes on the door. She'd passed him when his voice stopped her.

'I felt guilty. That's why I pulled back. I wanted

to give you space.'

'Space?' She frowned, tested the word on her tongue. 'Why would I need space?' Was this some convoluted way of giving her the brush off without saying he just didn't want her – as his assistant, or in bed, anymore?

'You know why. I should never have taken you to bed.'

Allegra's heart stalled then, finally, stuttered into action. So there it was. 'Because you didn't want to ruin a good working relationship.'

'No, damn it! Because you were vulnerable!' His out-of-control tone, so unfamiliar, had her spinning around. To her amazement she barely recognised Luca. He looked…distressed, like metal hammered too thin.

'I apologised but it wasn't enough. You were a virgin!' His voice rose.

'And so? Are you saying women aren't able to decide when to lose their virginity?'

'Of course not.' His hand sliced the air between them. 'But you were hurting. For all I know that accident might have impaired your thinking. And I kept topping up your wineglass that night. You might have had concussion but I was too wrapped up in my own damned pleasure I didn't stop to think about that till it was too late.'

'You're telling me all this…' Allegra waved a hand to encompass them and the office. 'Your behaviour this week is because you decided you'd taken advantage of me?' She didn't know whether to be relieved or annoyed. Annoyed won out.

'I don't believe you, Luca. This *is* the twenty-first century, isn't it? Medical science has proved women can think for themselves.'

Already he was shaking his head. 'But I should never have—'

'Oh, listen to yourself! I'm a grown woman and I chose to have sex with you. All right?' Her voice rose from terse to strident. 'Just accept it and move on. I'm not some medieval maiden who's going to wither away because she touched a man.'

Her breasts rose and fell with each quickened breath and she saw his attention drop to the movement. It was the final straw. 'And just because I've had sex doesn't mean my brain's disappeared or I can't work anymore. If my presence bothers you, then say so. Don't cut me out of the loop. I've worked hard in this job and I deserve your respect.'

'Finished?'

Silently she nodded. Wow! Fury was far better than tears. She still hurt right down to her bones, but she'd far rather face Luca in a row than slink away and cry. That would come soon enough.

'I do respect you.'

Allegra snorted and was surprised when he grinned and moved closer.

'I missed you in Rome.' His voice dropped to that rich, dark chocolate tone that did crazy things to her insides. 'I wanted you in the boardroom, covering my back.' His mouth curled slowly, oh-so-slowly, into a sexy grin. 'And I wanted you in my bed, covering me any way you wanted.'

Allegra's mouth sagged open and a warm finger under her chin lifted it closed.

'Nothing to say, sweet Allegra?' Gone was the tension she'd read earlier. Luca de Laurentis looked exactly what he was, a powerful, sexy man, completely in control of that elemental charisma that had turned far too many women's heads. Including hers.

Well, he wasn't getting away with it.

'What am I supposed to say, Luca? That now you deign to decide I can survive the thrill of it, you'll let me back into your bed?'

The man had the temerity to toss back his head and laugh. Laugh! She'd always known he was a macho Italian male, but this was the limit.

Allegra swung around and marched to the door.

She got precisely three steps when his big hand on her shoulder stopped her in her tracks. Next thing she knew he'd spun her round and crowded her up against the end of her desk.

'I'm not laughing at you, *bella*. I'm laughing with pure joy. The future has never looked so bright.'

Despite her indignation she blinked up at him, questioning.

Suddenly his smile faded and he was all seriousness. His hand on her shoulder wove a feather light caress down her bare arm, evoking a storm of goose bumps.

'I want you back in my bed, Allegra. I've never wanted anything more. But I was scared to push in case I'd overstepped the mark. When you told me what had happened in London, and I thought back over my own behaviour...' He shrugged. 'I thought it better not to crowd you this week, but give you time to consider.'

'Consider what?' Allegra saw the look in his eyes and her stomach did a spiralling loop the loop.

'Me.' He captured her hand and pushed it against his chest so she felt the hard whack of his heart against his ribs. 'I want you in my life, Allegra, not just in my office.'

She drew a trembling breath as the fire in her belly doused. She was staring up at a man who looked as grave as if he stood on the edge of a precipice, except the light in his eyes spoke of hope, not despair.

'I'm sorry if I overreacted.'

'If?' She bit back a smile.

He offered a crooked smile that cracked her defences. 'It seems you bring out the protective side of me.'

She shook her head. 'I didn't know you had one.'

'Only towards my family.' He leaned closer. 'And now you.' His breath was sweet and warm on her face, a kiss of air.

'What, exactly, do you want from me, Luca?' Her heart was pounding so hard it was a miracle he didn't hear it.

'I want you to work with me. But more than that, I want you as my lover. For so long I've been attracted to the Allegra Davis I thought I knew, then I realised I'd barely scratched the surface.' He grabbed her hand and raised it to his lips. 'Now I want all of you, the clever, organised Ms Davis in the office and the abandoned, sexy Allegra in my bed. And not just in my bed. I want to take you white water rafting, and motor racing and all the other things I know we'll enjoy together. If you're brave enough, in time I'd like to introduce you to my family too.'

Allegra stared. It was all so close to her own dreams, it didn't seem real.

He paused, swallowing hard. 'I know it seems

sudden but I want you to give us a chance. I believe together we could build something special. Something long term.'

He bent his head and kissed her hand and she threaded her fingers through his thick, dark locks, loving the feel of him.

'I think you're right.'

'You do?' The excitement in his face was better than any thrill she'd ever got from racing a motor bike or hang gliding.

Allegra nodded. 'I think we could have something very special.' She'd already fallen for him, hook, line and sinker. And the way he spoke – surely that was man-speak for love? Or something very close to it. Anticipation filled her at the prospect of what lay ahead.

'I've only got one condition.' Allegra saw him stiffen at her words and felt her lips curve.

'What is it?'

'That you don't treat me like porcelain again. I'm a flesh and blood woman and I make up my own mind. Understood?'

'Understood.' He looked down at her for the longest time, until finally his lips curved up in a devilish grin.

'What is it?' This time she was the one hesitating.

Until she felt his hands at her waist, lifting her onto the desk. A second later he stepped into the V of her legs, sliding one hand slowly, oh-so-slowly up her thigh and sending trails of fire through her veins.

'I'm thinking of all the thrilling things I'd like to do with my flesh and blood lover. *If* she's willing.'

Allegra shot a glance past his broad shoulder to

the closed office door. No-one would ever enter without invitation. Besides, hadn't she vowed to stop living so sedately and enjoy more thrills?

For answer she tugged his head to hers and kissed him full on the mouth till he groaned and gathered her close.

After that there wasn't any time for thought as Allegra and Luca gave themselves up to the passion that would stay with them the rest of their lives.

IF YOU ENJOYED THIS STORY please tell your friends or consider writing a review.

YOU MIGHT ALSO LIKE OTHERS IN THIS SERIES:

HOT ITALIAN NIGHTS ANTHOLOGY 2,
BOOKS 4-6
The Italian's Bold Reckoning
At the Italian's Bidding
Falling for the Brooding Italian

BOOK SEVEN –
The Italian's Marriage Bargain

BOOK EIGHT –
Burning for the Italian

For other Annie West titles visit
www.annie-west.com

About Annie

ANNIE WEST LOVES WRITING SEXY, emotional stories about charismatic heroes and strong heroines, and not just because it gives her a chance to ignore housework! She is a USA Today Bestselling author, published in 25 languages, and has won the Romantic Times Reviewers' Choice Award and the Romance Writers of Australia Romantic Book of the Year.

She lives on the east coast of Australia between wonderful beaches and glorious wine country. When not writing and avoiding housework she can be found walking, enjoying good food and good company, travelling or reading. Annie loves chatting with readers as far apart as Brisbane, Bremen and Bermuda.

Visit Annie at *www.annie-west.com*

Sign up for her reader newsletter for advance notice of new releases, giveaways and behind the scenes info via her website.

Or follow her on Facebook at
www.facebook.com/anniewest.author

www.ingramcontent.com/pod-product-compliance
Lightning Source LLC
Chambersburg PA
CBHW071554110726
47908CB00007B/2103